"Police!" Levi called out. "Is anybody in the house?"

A woman screamed, "Help me!" from behind a closed door.

He moved toward the door. "Who's in there?"

"Show me your badge and police ID," the woman demanded.

He could tell she was terrified by the trembling in her voice.

"You'll see them when you see me."

The door opened a couple of inches. He saw a small woman with platinum blond curls. Her blue eyes, wide with fear, focused first on his face, then on the area behind him and then finally on the badge pinned to his chest.

"It's all right," he said. "I'm here to help you."

She opened the door all the way.

"Are you hurt?" he asked. There were reddish marks on her chin and cheek.

"I'm all right."

"What happened?"

"Somebody chased me with a hammer. He told me to get out of town or get buried here."

Jenna Night comes from a family of Southern-born natural storytellers. Her parents were avid readers and the house was always filled with books. No wonder she grew up wanting to tell her own stories. She's lived on both coasts, but currently resides in the Inland Northwest, where she's astonished by the occasional glimpse of a moose, a herd of elk or a soaring eagle.

Books by Jenna Night

Love Inspired Suspense

Last Stand Ranch
High Desert Hideaway
Killer Country Reunion
Justice at Morgan Mesa

Visit the Author Profile page at Harlequin.com for more titles.

Justice at Morgan Mesa

Jenna Night

HARLEQUIN® LOVE INSPIRED® SUSPENSE

Recycling programs for this product may not exist in your area.

ISBN-13: 978-1-335-67879-9

Justice at Morgan Mesa

This edition published by arrangement with Love Inspired Books.

www.Harlequin.com

Printed in U.S.A.

Thou wilt keep him in perfect peace, whose mind is stayed on thee: because he trusteth in thee.

—*Isaiah* 26:3

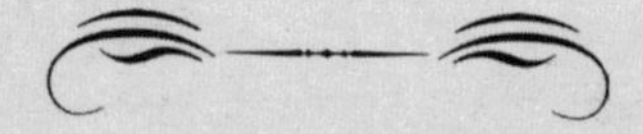

To my mother, Esther. A source of laughter and strength.

ONE

Vanessa Ford heard footsteps behind her. She turned around, but she didn't see anyone. Just pine forest beyond a narrow expanse of rocky soil and scraggly grass struggling to come back to life after a harsh winter.

Morgan Mesa, the place where she stood, towered a thousand feet above her hometown of Torchlight, Nevada. As a kid growing up in Torchlight, she'd been in awe of the rich people who lived on the rim of the mesa. The homes up here had looked like palaces to a little girl living in a single-wide trailer down on the flatland below. Since then she'd made something of herself as an attorney in Las Vegas, nearly five hundred miles away in the southern end of the state.

She was back in town for a few weeks to help her grandfather with preparations to open the Silver Horse Guest Ranch. He and his two closest friends had put their life savings into the endeavor. When their financing had come up short, Vanessa had kicked in some of her own money.

And while she was here, she was investigating a murder.

Standing at the edge of the mesa, she was sure she could feel someone's gaze focused on her. A chilly breeze brushed the surface of her skin, setting the hairs on the back of her neck on end.

Snap.

The sound of a footstep breaking a twig confirmed her suspicion. Somebody was there, hidden in the forest.

A weird whistling sound pierced the quiet. Vanessa tried to convince herself the noise had been made by an animal or some kind of machine. But she knew better. Somebody was hiding in the woods, whistling a creepy melody she couldn't quite place. Was someone deliberately trying to scare her? Her gut twisted itself into a knot and her heart began to race. Maybe she was on the verge of stumbling across something she wasn't meant to see.

The whistling sound abruptly stopped and the sudden quiet made Vanessa's racing heart pound even harder.

Her hands shook as she reached into her jeans pocket for her phone. She glanced toward the edge of the forest where she'd last heard the whistling, but she still couldn't see anyone.

She held her breath and listened for sounds of somebody moving around. Whoever was hiding in the woods, watching her, could make their move at any minute. If they were armed, they could fire a shot at her without ever leaving the cover of the forest.

She didn't have a weapon. Her car was parked a mile away. And the hiking boots she wore weren't designed for running. Her best option was to call the police and pray they got here fast.

She'd already started punching in 9-1-1 on her phone when she glanced down at the screen. Her heart sank. No bars. No cell service. She was on her own.

She was also still close to the rim of the mesa with a one-thousand-foot drop straight down. She could not stay there. Not if some lunatic was watching her with evil intentions in mind. The rustling of the breeze through the tops of the pine trees could easily mask the sound of footsteps. Maybe the creepy whistler had moved around and was no longer in the direction of where she'd last heard him.

In the late afternoon's blue-gray shadows, she couldn't see if anyone was there. Whichever direction she went, she ran the risk of running directly into the lurker she was trying to avoid.

There was always the chance that it was just some fool with a twisted sense of humor taking a shortcut through the woods. Maybe he was already gone.

Or maybe not.

"Hello?" she called out. "Anybody there?"

Nothing.

And then, from among the trees, a mocking, exaggeratedly falsetto voice repeated her words. "Hello? Anybody there?"

Goose bumps dimpled the surface of Vanessa's skin. It was time for her to leave.

She had to go through the woods to get away from the edge of the mesa. So she started walking quickly, trying to aim herself away from the direction of where she'd heard the voice. She was afraid if she ran it would trigger the person stalking her to run after her.

She'd just stepped into the dim light of the forest when the strange mocking voice called out again, "Hello? Anybody there?" This time it was directly in front of her.

Vanessa stopped. Which way should she go?

Panic clawed up from her chest into her throat. Her heart pounded in her ears.

She looked down at the phone in her shaking hand. Still no coverage. She hit 9-1-1 anyway and held the phone to her ear. Nothing. Then she looked up and immediately wished she hadn't.

A figure stepped out from the shadows. He was dressed in jeans and a long-sleeved red-and-white flannel shirt. He'd pulled his black knit cap down low over his face until it nearly covered his eyes and had covered the bottom of his face with a faded blue bandanna. And he carried a claw hammer in his right hand, tapping the prongs against the palm of his left hand. Through the fabric covering his mouth, she could hear the muffled sound of laughter. And then in a raspy, whispery voice he called out, "Get out of town or get buried here."

He started stalking toward her.

Run!

No longer frozen in place, she took a couple of stumbling steps while trying to decide which way to go. Then she turned right and sprinted farther into the forest.

Sometimes it paid to be short. Running as fast as she could with her boots sinking into the pine straw and soft loam, at least she could duck under most of the tree branches without needing to slow down. She did a quick mental calculation and figured out if she kept going straight, she'd get to the road. Maybe somebody would drive by and she could flag them down for help.

Or maybe no one would drive by and running along the edge of the road would just make her an easier target for the lunatic with the hammer.

She needed a new plan. But what? She knew panic would cloud her judgment. She couldn't give in to it, even though she wanted to. She wanted to scream. She wanted to cry. But this was not the time. *Lord, help!*

Her car was parked in the driveway of Heaton House. It was farther away than the road, but it was a smarter choice. She veered in that direction.

Heaton House had been the height of luxury when it was built back in the late nineteenth century. Nowadays, the wealthy descendants of Alistair Heaton lived in Lake Tahoe and used it only as an occasional vacation home. Plans were in the works for turning it into a museum.

Nearly an hour ago, Vanessa had parked in the driveway before hiking out to the mesa. Other than parking on the side of the road, the house's driveway was the only place to leave a car before coming to enjoy the beautiful view of Torchlight.

She'd come back to this spot before heading back down to the ranch because she'd been thinking about her dad and missing him. And she always felt close to him up here.

But right now, her thoughts were one hundred percent focused on avoiding his fate. She would not fall victim to a killer the way her father had all those years ago. And that meant running to her car as quickly as possible and getting away.

Her lungs burned and she gasped for air as she ran. Stark terror kept her legs pumping as hard and as fast as she could move them, but she was losing speed. The ground beneath her feet was rough and muddy, bogging her down like grasping hands.

Her pursuer was closing in on her. She could hear him.

Her phone. When she'd first arrived at Heaton House, she'd used her phone to make a call while she sat in her parked car. The signal had been fine. Maybe she was close enough to that spot to get reception now. Making a call meant slowing down, but she was slowing down anyway.

She slid her hand into her pocket and pulled out her phone. She glanced at the screen and saw a solitary bar. Relief poured over her. One bar was all she needed.

Her toe snagged under a tree root and she fell forward, smacking her chin and cheek hard on the ground. Her phone flew out of her hand. When she opened her eyes, she couldn't see where it had landed.

Her heart sank. The fall had knocked the wind out of her and for a few panicked seconds she couldn't catch her breath.

Behind her, she heard laughter. Then whooping and hollering. Her tormentor was enjoying this. He probably could have caught her already if he'd wanted to. He was just dragging it out for fun.

Despite the pain from her fall, Vanessa felt her face grow hot with fury. Her anger shoved aside her fear. Yet, another strategy for survival became clearer. If dragging things out was what this jerk wanted, why not use his twisted sense of fun against him?

She pushed herself up to her hands and knees and glanced back. She could see the masked stalker coming after her but he wasn't running anymore. He was sauntering toward her, loosely swinging the claw hammer back and forth. He was that sure he had her.

Idiot.

Vanessa pushed herself up onto her feet and started a staggering jog toward Heaton House, which was now visible through the trees. She added a fake limp to keep her pursuer from chasing her any more aggressively. Let him keep making sport of the whole thing. If her plan worked, the fake limp would help her conserve energy for a final dash to her car.

If it didn't work, she was all out of plans.

When she thought she might be close enough to where she'd parked, she reached into her pocket for her key fob and hit the unlock button. Her car made a beeping sound that betrayed her plan. She hit the alarm button, too.

Then she ran full bore, no longer faking a limp.

She heard a howl of rage close behind her and the steel hammer flashed by, smacking hard against a tree just ahead of her and splitting the bark.

That tree could have been her head.

She finally reached the edge of the scruffy-looking lawn that surrounded Heaton House. Her only obstacles now were the decorative boulders lining the driveway. Once she was past them, she'd be safe. She could get into her car and tear out of here, down the road into town and directly to the Torchlight Police Department.

She made it past the decorative boulders and stopped so suddenly she nearly toppled over. Her heart fell to her feet as she looked at her car. All four of her tires had been slashed.

At least the alarm was still blaring. There were no other houses nearby, but maybe somebody would hear the alarm and call the police. Yet, she hated to count on a "maybe."

She turned to the house. It was nearing sunset and the exterior lights had turned on. The Heatons were so proud of this house and its role in their family history; it *had* to be connected to a security system. She would attempt to trigger the alarm.

She reached for the handle on the front door and tried to turn it. Of course, it was locked. It looked like there might be a security camera in the shadowy corner of the house on the other side of the front door, but she couldn't be certain.

She stepped back, grabbed a stone the size of a softball from the ground beside the front step and chucked it through a window. An alarm sounded. She quickly threw a couple more stones until the pane was nearly gone. She yanked off her suede jacket, threw it over the bottom of the windowsill and climbed over it.

She dropped into the house, crouched down and turned to peek out the bottom of the broken window.

She didn't see anyone. The man chasing her was out of sight. She let out a sigh. The blaring car and house alarms must have scared him away.

Something slammed into the front door beside her and she jumped. It hit again and again, and it didn't stop. It was the guy who was chasing her. If the psychopathic creep took a second to look around, he'd see the window she'd just broken and climb through it right after her. If he just kept pounding with that stupid hammer, he was bound to eventually break through the wooden door.

Either way, he had her.

Vanessa leaped to her feet and ran farther into the house. She'd never been inside before and didn't know which way to go. Just past the kitchen, she spotted an open door to what looked like a den and she ran for it. She slammed the door shut just as she heard the front door splinter and break open. There was no lock on the den door. She shoved a heavy end table in front of it as a barricade, fully aware it wouldn't keep the attacker out for long.

Then the hammer started pounding on the den door. It would break any second. And the psycho would get in.

Most likely a couple of bored high school kids had busted a window at the Heaton House and set off the alarm again.

Normally, some fresh-out-of-the-academy patrol officer would have been sent to respond, but Lieutenant Levi Hawk of the Torchlight Police Department had been in the neighborhood. So when the call came in, he keyed his radio mic and let dispatch know he'd respond himself.

He followed the main road across the back of Morgan Mesa as it wound through a stretch of forest dotted with modest houses and trailers. It wasn't as bustling as the town, but there were plenty of employees from the nearby O'Connell ranch who chose to live up here, along with a few other people who preferred the quieter setting. Property inland and away from the edge of the mesa overlooking Torchlight was actually reasonably priced and normal people could afford it. Roughly eight miles ahead, the road angled toward the dozen or so elaborate homes built closer to the mesa's rim, each one surrounded by a few acres of the homeowner's private forest, which was also the neighborhood where the Heaton House was located.

Dispatch contacted him again to add that they'd received a report of a blaring car alarm near the historic house. That was something different—something out of character for bored teens. Maybe this would turn out to be an interesting call after all. Levi sped up.

When he arrived at the house, he saw a gold sedan with four slashed tires parked in the driveway. The car's alarm was still blaring, but it sounded faint and gurgling, like the car's battery was dying down. Meanwhile, the house alarm, loud and shrill, was still going strong.

More important, the front door to the house was busted open and one of the windows was broken with some kind of cloth lying over the bottom of the frame. This didn't look like the work of kids just fooling around. He called for backup and then got out of his police department SUV.

Moving cautiously up the driveway, he scanned his surroundings. He didn't see anybody there, but a couple of tours with the marines in Iraq had taught him never to assume any situation was safe.

Continuing to move toward the house, he glanced into the sedan and saw a purse and a leather satchel on the front passenger-seat floor. Was the owner inside the house, injured or in danger? Had someone with bad intent broken down the door or climbed through the window after her? Levi drew his pistol and moved closer to the front door entrance.

A couple of security lights shone on the outside of the house, but inside it was filled with shadow. Plenty of places for someone to hide.

"Police!" Levi called out as he stepped past the broken door and crossed over the threshold. "Is anybody in the house?"

"Here!"

The shrieking house alarm made it hard for him to know which direction the shout had come from.

He scanned the area around him. The little bit of light coming through the windows shone on fragments of glass atop the hardwood floor. There was a trail of them that led from the broken window over to a closed door. Maybe someone in trouble was behind the door. Or maybe a bad guy wanted his attention focused on that closed door so he could attack Levi from a different direction.

"Police!" he called out again. "If anybody is in the house, show yourself!"

Over the shrill sound of the alarm, he heard something crash at the far end of the sprawling ranch house, followed by the sound of a door being yanked open. He'd already started in that direction when he heard a woman screaming, "Help me!" from behind the closed door. Drawing closer to it, he saw there were dents and cracks on it, as if whoever had broken down the front door had beaten on this one, too.

He wanted to give chase to the person who'd just fled, but he needed to check on the woman calling out for help first.

Still wary of a trap, he moved toward the door. "Who's in there?"

"Show me your badge and police ID," the woman demanded.

He could tell she was terrified by the trembling in her voice, but he admired the gumption she showed by standing her ground.

"You'll see them when you see me."

He turned the handle and pushed, but the door didn't move.

"Wait a minute," she called out.

It sounded like she was shoving aside something heavy. And then the door opened a couple of inches. He saw a small woman with platinum-blond curls. There were pine needles in her hair. Her chin and part of her cheek were covered with mud. Her blue eyes, wide with fear, focused first on his face, then on the area behind him and then finally on the badge pinned to his chest.

"It's all right," he said. "I'm here to help you." He was in uniform but to make her feel safe, he quickly showed her his ID.

She opened the door all the way.

"Are you hurt?" he asked. There were reddish marks on her chin and cheek.

She blew out a breath. "I'm all right." She pulled a key fob out of her pocket and turned off the car alarm.

"What happened?" He stepped back from the den into the dining area where he could have a better view of his surroundings. He'd been inside of the house before, but it had been a while.

"Some lunatic chased me with a hammer."

A *hammer*? That explained the busted-up front door.

"Do you know this person?"

She shook her head, then winced. He keyed his collar mic and called for EMS to respond. She didn't seem to be significantly injured, but it was possible that adrenaline was masking it. Better safe than sorry. He also asked for the alarm company to be contacted so the alarm could be remotely turned off and to log a request for them to send him whatever video footage they had.

"The man who chased me didn't identify himself, and he had his face covered," the woman said.

Levi holstered his gun, then pulled out a chair and gestured for her to sit down. He flipped on a light switch. "What's your name?" He had to raise his voice to be heard over the alarm.

"Vanessa—" She said her last name but it was drowned out by the blare of the alarm.

"I'm Lieutenant Levi Hawk," he responded loudly.

Suddenly the alarm stopped.

In the quiet few seconds that followed, the pinched, fearful expression on her face began to ease a little.

She took a fortifying breath and then told him a harrowing story about being chased to the house from the edge of the mesa. As she spoke, the dazed look in her eyes gave way to a more focused expression.

After she finished her story, two of his patrolmen arrived. He had them search the house.

"Why were you over by the edge of the mesa?" he asked. Any details she gave him might help him hunt down the bad guy.

Vanessa arched a pale blond eyebrow. "The Heatons allow the public to enjoy the view from their property along the mesa. They have for years."

She was defensive. That was interesting. Levi decided to prod a little more. "Why did you decide to enjoy the view *this* evening?"

She frowned at him for a moment, sighed and then glanced away. "I grew up around here. Moved away. I'm back for a short while and I wanted to visit a few of my old haunts."

"Where do you live now? What do you do?"

"Vegas. I'm a defense attorney."

Vanessa. A memory clicked into place in the back of Levi's mind. "What did you say your last name is?"

"Ford. My name is Vanessa Ford."

"Are you related to Josh Ford?"

She nodded, the expression in her eyes turning sorrowful. "Yes. He was my dad."

Levi glanced away and drew in a breath as memories tumbled through his mind. He'd just been twelve years old when Josh Ford's lifeless body was found on a lonely stretch of road up here on the mesa. It was the first major news story of his young life that he could remember paying attention to. His parents had talked about it at the time. Everybody had. Unease had settled over the town as the weeks and months and ultimately years had passed without the murderer being found.

Vanessa had been eight years old. He remembered seeing her picture. He especially remembered seeing the lost expression in her blue eyes. For weeks, he'd been worried that something terrible would happen to his own parents, until finally that anxiety had faded.

Vanessa had already had more than enough heartache for one lifetime. She didn't deserve to have some violent maniac chasing her.

So who was after her and why?

"Has anybody from your work threatened you?" Levi asked.

"No."

"Are you sure? You're a defense attorney. Hasn't anyone you've defended ever gone to prison? Maybe held a grudge against you that they intended to settle when they got out? Or what about an angry victim, or their family, who felt like you helped a bad guy go free?"

She blew out a sigh. "Of course I've been threatened a few times, blamed by one side or the other whether my client has been convicted or gone free. As a cop, I imagine you've been threatened, too. Most of the time it's just somebody blowing off steam."

"Sometimes those aren't empty threats. Think about it and see if you can think of some names for me to check out."

She nodded and tucked a few loose strands of hair behind her ear. It was still the same pale blond color it had been when she was a girl. Still very curly.

"Did the guy with the hammer say anything to you?" Levi asked.

"He told me to get out of town or get buried here."

"Get buried *here*, on this property? Is that what he meant?" Had she stumbled across someone illicitly using the house, doing something on the property that they wanted to remain undiscovered? There'd been talk recently of turning the house into a museum. Could someone want to sabotage that for some reason? Make people afraid to come up here?

"I don't know what exactly he meant by his stupid threat," she said irritably.

"Could you have crossed paths with him recently? Maybe you'd had a disagreement?"

"I've spent the last couple of days up here on the mesa, stopping in stores and cafés and different places, asking people if they knew or ever heard rumors about what happened to my dad. Nobody knew anything. It was all such a long time ago." She shook her head and winced again. "What happened tonight probably doesn't have anything to do with that. Maybe he's just some dealer cooking meth in the woods around here."

"Why are you conducting an investigation into your dad's murder now?" Levi asked, feeling his heart speed up a little at the thought that the case might finally be solved. "Do you have some new information?"

"No new information. This is just something I've thought about doing for a long time. And now I finally have the chance to do it."

Levi's cop instinct told him she wasn't telling him the whole truth, but this wasn't the time to press. He heard the ambulance pull up into the driveway and convinced her to let a medic take a look at her.

By the time she'd been cleared, his officers had completed their search of the house and hadn't found anyone hiding in there. He had one of them stay behind to take down basic contact information from Vanessa and make sure she got home safely. Then he grabbed a couple of flashlights from his SUV and had the other officer go with him to look for signs of the chase she'd described and to search for whatever evidence they could find.

He didn't know what he expected to find, especially in the dark, but he knew he wouldn't feel comfortable leaving until he'd done everything he could. Levi had experienced a rocky return to the United States after his years spent fighting overseas. When he'd finally made his way back to Torchlight, he'd become a police officer to give something back to his hometown and do something to help heal his soul. Protecting Vanessa and capturing the sick assailant who'd attacked her would help him fulfill both of those goals.

Maybe this weird attack was related to Josh Ford's murder all those years ago. Maybe not.

TWO

"You have to tell your grandfather what happened to you tonight."

"Of course I will." Vanessa glanced over at the woman riding in the pickup truck's passenger seat, Rosa Sandoval. Her husband, Pablo, had worked as a ranch hand alongside Vanessa's grandfather for years.

When Vanessa's grandparents started looking into buying property and turning it into a guest ranch for their working retirement, it naturally followed that they'd invite their best friends to join in the venture. Pablo and Rosa had jumped at the chance.

"I'm not trying to deceive Grandpa. I would never do that." Vanessa downshifted her grandfather's old truck when she came to a steep drop in the road. "It's just that he's finally gotten back to his normal sleeping pattern. It's been eight months since Grandma Katherine passed away and for most of that time, I don't think he slept more than two or three hours a night."

"For a while there, he really was looking like something the cat dragged home," Rosa agreed.

"Now that he's finally back to his usual routine of lights out at eight at night and coffee in his cup by four the next morning, I don't want to mess that up by having him worry about me tonight. He needs his rest."

Rosa sighed loudly. "You *have* to tell him as soon as you get up tomorrow morning."

"Yes, ma'am, I will. And I'll call my mom and let her know what happened, too."

Vanessa glanced over and offered her a smile. Rosa was a retired parole officer, which meant she could be tough when she needed to be. Just the kind of person Vanessa wanted alongside her on the ride home tonight.

With a borrowed phone from a patrolman, Vanessa had called to have her car towed into town so the tires could be replaced and the battery checked out. Then she'd called Rosa, at the time telling her only that she'd had car trouble and needed a ride back to the ranch.

Vanessa shifted gears again when they reached the foot of the mesa and drove back onto flat land. She'd wanted to do the driving because she'd thought it would help her feel more in control. So far, it hadn't worked. The stuff of nightmares had just happened to her. A masked lunatic had tried to kill her. With a *hammer.*

Thank You, Lord, for protecting me.

A cold chill passed over the surface of her skin and she drew in a quivering breath.

Rosa reached forward and turned on the heater.

After a few seconds, warm air blew out, relaxing Vanessa's tense muscles. In a way, it made things worse. Physically relaxing made her emotions start to loosen up, and she became more conscious of them. That was the last thing she wanted right now.

What she needed to do was toughen up and pull herself together. She'd done that as a kid when her father was murdered. And again, when her mother had gotten remarried to an abusive man and it had seemed like life was just one terrible thing happening after another. She'd gone on to hone that skill of tamping down her true emotions when she became a lawyer and needed to appear confident every time she stepped into a courtroom.

"I saw Levi Hawk while I was sitting in the

truck waiting for you," Rosa said. "He's a very determined and thorough investigator." Despite her retirement, Rosa still kept active ties to the law enforcement community.

"Good to know," Vanessa said. He was handsome, too. Military-cut black hair. Intelligent dark eyes. Bronze skin. And a capable, calm demeanor. Not that any of that mattered.

Vanessa tapped her thumbs on the steering wheel, directing her thoughts back to the man who'd chased her tonight, trying to think of any hint at who he was or what his motive might be. She'd been threatened a few times during the course of her career, but never anything like this. She couldn't imagine it was connected to her work back in Vegas. Her attacker had seemed intent on getting her away from here, specifically. Why would a client with a grudge care where she went?

"What I'm wondering is whether that guy knew you were going to be up on the Heaton property and was waiting for you," Rosa said. "Or if you were just in the wrong place at the wrong time and stumbled across some creep who was desperate to scare you away for some reason. Did you tell anybody you were going to be there?"

"Yeah. Pretty much everybody I talked to

on the mesa today. I had no reason to think it was dangerous to do that. I know it was a long shot, but I guess I was hoping somebody might come out and join me to tell me something new about my dad. Maybe give me some new information on what happened to him twenty years ago. I let people know I was going to be there on the Heaton property because I wanted to make it easy for anyone who didn't want to talk to me around other people, or who might be afraid of our conversation being recorded if they talked to me on the phone."

Rosa turned in her seat to face Vanessa. "Well, you need to make sure you don't go to some isolated place alone again. Not until this creep is caught. And don't tell strangers where you're going to be."

Vanessa felt herself trembling again. She glanced in the rearview mirror to see if they were being followed. Of course they were. They were on the only road that led down from the mesa and it intersected with the four-lane highway heading into Torchlight. You could eventually get into Torchlight by following the unpaved county roads on the mesa, but it would add a good sixty miles to the trip. She tried not to be bothered by the headlights behind her, but she felt her shoulders tighten up all the same.

"I'll be very careful from now on, believe me," Vanessa muttered, understanding the wisdom of the advice but still angered that she had to change what she did because of some violent crazy person.

They were nearing the intersection with the highway. Torchlight was to the left. The Silver Horse Guest Ranch—her grandfather's new home—was to the right, several miles away.

"I bet you haven't had dinner," Rosa said. "We could load you up with pancakes and hot chocolate. All those carbs will make you sleepy."

"I'm too nervous to eat anything."

"Honey, I've been through some pretty hair-raising situations in my day," Rosa said. "And my experience is that afterward you need some time with somebody you can talk to. Even if you don't eat, you need to talk until you start to wind down a little. Then maybe when you get back to the ranch, you'll be able to fall asleep."

Vanessa doubted she would get any sleep tonight. She was pretty sure anytime she closed her eyes she'd see that masked figure with that claw hammer and hear him laughing. She wanted to put that experience off for as long as she could.

"Okay," she said, turning left onto the highway. "Let's go into town."

The next morning, Levi turned off the highway at the sign that read Silver Horse Guest Ranch. He drove up the winding private road, early-morning sunlight filtering through the new spring leaves on the trees lining the way.

This was an unannounced visit after last night's strange attack up on Morgan Mesa. Between searching the area on and around the Heaton property for any evidence he could find and coordinating a search for the suspect, Levi hadn't had as much time as he'd wanted to interview Vanessa. He hadn't found the perpetrator last night and he was anxious to get the investigation moving forward today. The creep who liked to threaten women with a hammer needed to be locked up.

Sometimes after a vicious attack, when a little time had passed, people remembered helpful details they hadn't mentioned before. There was also the possibility that Vanessa had withheld some important bit of information intentionally last night, either because it was embarrassing or because it might incriminate her in some illegal activity. Levi wanted to talk to her while she was still a little off-balance from the attack and might find it difficult to hide the truth.

His police SUV rattled as he drove over a cattle guard. The noise might wake up some of the ranch's vacationing guests, but that would just add to the authenticity of their visit. From his own ranching childhood, he knew waking up early was an integral part of an authentic ranch experience.

The Silver Horse Guest Ranch was sixteen miles east of town on what used to be a family-owned horse ranch. The family's younger generation had sold out, and apparently the buyer had turned it into a guest ranch. Vanessa had told the patrol officer he'd handed her off to last night that she was staying here.

After driving through a couple of curves in the winding dirt road, the view opened up to a fenced meadow on the left and a sprawling ranch house on the right. Beyond the ranch house, scattered among the trees, he spotted several small unfinished cabins. It looked like the guest ranch wasn't open for business yet.

A big blue storage trailer sat alongside the private drive with piles of raw lumber and paint cans stacked against it. The stables were tucked up fairly close to the ranch house with a big red barn and a couple of other storage buildings a little farther away.

Levi parked his SUV in front of the ranch house and walked up the three steps to the wide front porch. There were four rocking chairs sitting out there, each one a different style and color. An ancient-looking calico cat occupied one cushioned seat. She lifted her head and slowly blinked as he walked up. He reached out to pat her head, half expecting her to run away before he could touch her. But she didn't.

After scratching the orange patch between her ears for a few seconds, he glanced up. The drapes were open at a pair of large windows beside the front door, and he could see Vanessa Ford inside seated in a straight-backed wooden chair, an elbow propped on the dining table beside it and her forehead pressed into the palm of her other hand.

Across from her, a tall, sinewy man in dark jeans and a long-sleeved Western shirt paced back and forth. His hair was mostly steel gray with a few black streaks while his thick mustache was almost completely black. He waved both of his arms as he talked. "You should have woken me up and told me!"

Levi was interrupting an argument. It sounded like it was about the attack on her last night. He stood by the window so they'd be able to see him, then reached over and knocked on the door.

The man looked at him first. His face was red. Then Vanessa lifted her head to look toward him. The red marks he'd seen on her chin and the side of her face after she'd tripped and fallen last night had darkened into purple bruises. The man strode over to open the door and Levi introduced himself.

"Sam Ford," the man said in response. "Come on in, Lieutenant. I believe I have you to thank for saving my granddaughter's life." With that, he turned to glare at Vanessa.

Vanessa shifted her gaze to Levi. Her eyes were squinted like she was in pain. Maybe a headache. He'd fallen and smacked his head a few times and he knew how she felt. He also understood the alternating emotions of buoyant relief and sinking terror once the adrenaline wore off after someone tried to kill you.

Not that he was convinced the man who attacked her last night had truly intended to kill her. If so, she'd be dead now. The attack was almost theatrical. Fear was the goal. Now he needed some leads on who would do that to her and why.

"Sorry to interrupt your morning," Levi said as he stepped inside. They were in a dining area. Wood floors, oak table and chairs, a couple of potted plants, coffee mugs hanging from pegs on the wall, and not much else. The current residents hadn't been settled in for very long. "I came out to ask Ms. Ford a few questions."

"You could have just phoned me," she grumbled, running a fingernail up and down the handle of her coffee mug. "And call me Vanessa."

"I wasn't aware you'd gotten your phone back."

Her shoulders dropped and she sighed. "I haven't."

"We've got a good group of volunteers working with a couple of officers up on the mesa. They're doing a second search of the Heaton property now that it's daylight. If your phone is still up there, they'll find it."

Levi felt another presence walk into the room and turned to see a second older gentleman, this one shorter than Mr. Ford, with sparse reddish hair. He was barrel-shaped and wearing a white cook's apron. He walked from the kitchen area with a plate of muffins and a coffeepot. He set the muffins on the table and turned to Levi. "Good morning. Would you like some coffee?"

"Sure, thanks."

"This is Pablo Sandoval," Vanessa said. "Pablo, this is Lieutenant Levi Hawk."

"Pleased to meet you," Pablo said as he took a mug from a peg on the wall and filled it with coffee for Levi. "I'm grateful to God that you arrived at that house in time to keep something terrible from happening to Vanessa."

Levi nodded. He was a praying man. And he, too, was grateful to God that nothing worse had happened.

"This is Rosa," Vanessa added, making the introductions as a lady with graying hair pulled back into a tight bun walked into the room and smiled at him.

"Rosa and I know each other through work," Levi said. "It's good to see you."

This wasn't the first time he'd had to intrude on a family while doing his job. He'd accepted the offer of coffee in an attempt to be social, which wasn't always his strong suit. But he'd been working on it. He thought about forcing a friendly smile on his face, but didn't. His sister, Angela, told him he looked scary when he did that. "How are you feeling?" he asked Vanessa.

"Probably about how I look. Bruised."

"Why bother asking?" her grandfather

snapped. "She'll just tell you everything's fine. She won't be forthcoming."

Pablo loudly cleared his throat and gestured toward the plate he'd set on the table. "Applesauce muffins. Anybody hungry?"

Apparently, nobody was. No one made a move toward the food. Everyone's attention was focused on Vanessa.

"So, you live in Las Vegas and your family lives here?" Levi asked her.

Vanessa started to nod, winced and stopped. "We bought this property a few months ago. There's still a lot of work to be done before the guest ranch opens for business."

"Do you have any leads on who attacked my granddaughter?" Sam asked impatiently.

"Not yet." Levi watched Vanessa closely, trying to gauge whether she was holding back information. Maybe she didn't want to talk in front of her grandfather. "I have several questions for you," he added. "Maybe you'd like to step outside. We could talk on your porch."

"You can talk right here," Sam growled out. He pulled out a chair for Levi and one for himself. Pablo and Rosa headed off into the kitchen area. There was the sound of a cabinet door opening and a bag rattling. A gray tabby cat shot down the staircase beside the dining area and disappeared into the kitchen, heading toward the sound of kibble being poured into a bowl.

"Good morning, Tornado," Levi could hear Pablo saying in the kitchen.

"Vanessa should have called me last night right after everything happened," her grandpa said, his voice a low rumble, leaving no room for argument. He twisted in his chair to face her. "We would have gone to the hospital to have you checked out. Maybe had you stay there overnight just to be certain you were all right." He shook his head. "No more secrets, little girl. Not with me."

"I'm sorry, Grandpa." Vanessa's eyes looked watery and her nose reddened. She sniffed loudly, then turned to Levi. "Go ahead and ask your questions—it's fine for us to stay in here."

"First, have you thought of anything else to tell me about the events last night? Anything you remembered?"

"Not really. I've tried to think of anything I could add to the physical description of the guy who chased me, but I can't."

"That's all right. Maybe you'll see or hear something later that will trigger a memory. Meanwhile, you mentioned being up on the mesa to talk to people about your dad. I'll need a list of the names of the people you spoke to."

"I can give you the names of people I know that I've spoken to since I've been back in town. But when it comes to the people I spoke to on the mesa yesterday, I don't know their names. They were strangers. Out of desperation to generate a lead, I took a chance and I just stopped at random places. A couple of gas stations, a coffee shop. The Carson Family Diner. I told people who I was and asked if they knew anything about my dad and what happened to him. Asked if they had any theories or ever heard any rumors about who'd murdered him or why."

"Did anybody have anything to tell you?"

"No. I gave people my phone number in case they thought of something. And I mentioned I was going to stop at the edge of the mesa on the Heaton property and enjoy the view around sundown before I headed back down to the flatland." She drew in a shaky breath.

"I'll need a list of the places where you stopped to talk to people," Levi said. "And the names of anyone back in Vegas who might be angry with you. Disgruntled clients. People who are upset because you successfully defended someone who they thought should have been convicted. Jealous colleagues, bitter exes—whatever you can think of. It's all worth looking into. And if you can think of anyone who physically reminds you of the man who attacked you, add that name to the list, too. We'll check them all out."

Levi could almost physically feel how desperately this family wanted answers. Right now, though, he couldn't give them any.

Sam cleared his throat and squared his shoulders. Levi could see the frustration in the older man's eyes, along with the fear that had likely triggered the dressing-down he'd been giving his granddaughter when Levi first arrived.

"Are you familiar with what happened to Vanessa's father?" Sam asked. "You would have been a kid at the time it happened, but you still might remember. It was all over the news."

"I did grow up here, sir. I remember very well when it happened and I'm sorry for your loss. I want you to know I'll definitely be investigating that angle, but I can't assume what happened on the mesa last night is related to your son's murder. I need to keep an open mind and collect as much information as I can."

"Along with the other places I mentioned, I also stopped by the O'Connell ranch, where my dad was employed when he was murdered," Vanessa added. She glanced at her grandpa. "Mr. O'Connell wasn't there. Neither was his son, Trent. I talked to a couple of ranch hands, but neither of them were employed at the ranch back when the murder happened." She leaned back in her chair and crossed her arms. "It's hard to believe that my asking simple questions after all this time would get somebody upset enough to attack me. Nobody had anything useful to tell me. Maybe it really is related to something back in Las Vegas. Or something I accidentally stumbled across."

"Why are you asking people about your dad *now*?" Levi asked. When he'd asked her last night about the timing of her investigation, her answer had been vague. Now he wanted specifics. "This can't be the only time you've come back to town to visit since you moved away."

"I've thought about coming home, asking questions and trying to stir up interest in my dad's murder case before, but I never had the nerve to do it. Not that I ever thought anyone would attack me," she quickly added. "I suppose I was afraid I'd learn something about my dad I didn't really want to know. Or that I'd hear some new detail about how he died or what his body was like when he was found that would give me nightmares."

Levi felt a sympathetic twinge in the pit of his stomach. He could imagine the horrible nightmares she'd had about her father's murder over the years. The terrible things she'd imagined when a dark mood settled over her. He'd experienced all of those things and more due to his combat experience. He knew the raw feeling a person was left with in the aftermath.

"So why did you decide to go through with it now?" he asked.

"My grandmother passed away recently. And that reminded me that I'm running out of time to find someone who might know what happened. At some point, any potential witnesses will pass on, too, and I'll never be able to get an answer to the question of who murdered my father."

"It's not your job to find the killer," Sam said, focusing his gaze on his granddaughter.

Vanessa reached for her coffee mug and took a sip. "It's not anyone's job, anymore—no one's looked into it in years. If I don't find answers, who will? I do some investigative work for my job, but I'm not a professional investigator," she said to Levi. "But I thought maybe I could get some small piece of information, something that changes the timeline of events or brings somebody's alibi into question, and I'd pass that along to the police. Anything to make my dad's cold case active again."

"Are you telling me you haven't gotten that little bit of information you're looking for yet?"

She opened her mouth as if to answer, then closed it and looked thoughtful for a moment. "I'd forgotten about this until just now, but about midday yesterday I stopped to get something for lunch and my phone rang. I answered it, but whoever it was hung up. I remember the number was the local area code and prefix but I didn't have a name associated with it in my contact list. I called back, hoping it was someone I'd talked to earlier who wanted to speak to me in private, but no one answered. I suppose it could have just been a misdialed number. But maybe not."

Levi took out his phone and tapped the screen a couple of times. "What's your phone number?"

She told him and he entered it into his phone. "Obviously we don't have your phone," he said. "But that incoming call should be listed in your phone records. I'll check with the phone company and see what we can find out about whoever called you."

"All right." She nodded her agreement. Her shoulders slumped forward.

Levi could tell her energy was running low. And with good reason. She'd been through a lot last night, and probably hadn't slept well.

He pulled a business card out of his shirt pocket and handed it to her. "Here's my contact information. Email me a list of all the potential suspects you can think of from Vegas, as well as the names of the businesses where you stopped to talk to people up on the mesa. I'd like that by this afternoon." He really wanted that information right now, but if he put too much pressure on her, he was afraid she might accidentally leave out something important.

"I'll get all of that to you as soon as possible," she said, taking his card. "But I've got a meeting with our accountant downtown at one o'clock today to go over some things, so we can get this guest ranch up and running on schedule. I can't miss that."

"The accountant can wait," her grandpa said firmly, but Vanessa shook her head, not backing down.

"I've got to keep that appointment." Vanessa glanced at Levi. "My boss is expecting me back at work in a couple of weeks. I've got a schedule of things I want to accomplish while I'm here in Torchlight and I need to stick to it. But I'll make sure I get you that information today."

"Thank you." Levi got to his feet.

Sam Ford also stood and reached out to shake Levi's hand. "Thank you again for helping my granddaughter. You come out here and ask questions anytime you need to."

Levi nodded. "Thank you, sir. I will."

Vanessa walked him to the door. When she pulled it open, the old calico cat that had been sitting in the rocking chair made a surprisingly fast dash into the house and toward the kitchen. Clearly, she knew where the feline breakfast was being served.

Vanessa smiled as the cat ran by her feet. Seeing that smile on a face marked by bruises made Levi's chest ache. Vanessa had already suffered through so much. But apparently somebody wanted her to suffer even more.

"When you go into town this afternoon, don't go alone," he said as he headed down the steps.

"I'll be careful," she assured him.

"Good."

Once he was clear of the porch, he stopped, turned and waited for her to go back into the house and shut the door.

The problem with being careful was that sometimes it simply wasn't enough. You couldn't predict every single thing that could go wrong. He'd learned that in a war zone overseas. He'd witnessed it again as a cop after he came home.

If someone was willing to attack Vanessa with a hammer, there was no telling what they might do next. And no way to be prepared for their next move.

THREE

Vanessa was once again behind the wheel of her grandfather's reliable old truck. Just like last night, she hoped that driving would give her a sense of control as she steered it into town. So far it actually had helped her calm down a little. And it gave her mind something to do other than replay the terrifying scenes from last night.

"Maybe I should scrap my plans and stick with you," Rosa said as Vanessa pulled into a parking space and left the engine idling.

Grandpa had wanted to come with them, but Vanessa eventually convinced him to stay at the ranch. Physical work would calm him down, which was exactly what he needed and what Vanessa wanted. Plus, Rosa had her pistol. She could protect Vanessa quite adequately if it came to that.

"Rosa, I'll be fine." Vanessa's response came

out sounding like a snarl. That was not her intention. She tried again. "You're just making excuses so you don't have to let Marisol Beltran's granddaughter show you a thing or two about technology," she added, while focusing on making her tone sound lighter and putting an awkward smile on her lips.

Truly, she was grateful to Rosa for accompanying her into Torchlight, but she didn't want to be coddled. She wanted the long list of tasks assigned to everyone to be completed on time so they could open the Silver Horse Guest Ranch on schedule.

Rosa had already made arrangements for today to meet with a technology coach to get help upgrading the simple website she'd set up to include an online reservations system. She'd been miffed to discover her "coach" was only twenty years old and the granddaughter of a friend. Rosa had held her when she was a baby and that didn't seem all that long ago.

Rosa opened the door, but instead of getting out she turned to Vanessa. "Maybe instead of you dropping me off, I should drive you to the accountant's office and make sure you get inside safely."

Vanessa took a deep breath and squeezed the steering wheel as tight as she could before releasing it. It was a tension-relieving technique she'd learned years ago and at the moment it was helping a little.

She understood the concern behind Rosa's offer, but having her loved ones hover just made her feel more anxious. Of course she was afraid. Every time she'd glanced at the truck's mirrors on the drive over she'd seen the dark purple bruises. A reminder that if Levi hadn't shown up when he had, her night could have had a far worse ending.

But she was determined not to let fear paralyze her. She'd seen what had happened to her mother after her father's death. And again, after her mom had married a man whose attitude and behavior were poisonous.

Vanessa did pro bono legal work for women living in a shelter in Las Vegas. And as so often happens, in helping others she'd received more than she'd given away. Among other things, she'd heard counselors talk to the women about being cautious and safe, but also about doing their best to not let anxiety torment them and create a stronghold in their minds.

Vanessa was *not* going to let some idiot with a hammer torment her. She was not going to let some violent jerk control her the way her stepfather had controlled her mother.

She would be cautious. Smart. Reasonable.

"I'll be fine," she said to Rosa, managing to keep her tone light and easy. "I'm going to the accountant's office and then by the library. And the police station is smack in the middle of town so it's close to both places. Everything will be fine. Now, you get in there and learn something about the exciting world of online reservations processing."

Rosa hesitated for a few seconds before finally nodding in agreement and exiting.

Vanessa steered the truck back onto the road, drove a couple of blocks over and found an open spot where she could park on the street directly in front of the public library. She cut the engine and sent her grandpa a text, as promised, on the phone Pablo had lent her, letting him know she had arrived safely.

And then, sitting alone in the truck, she realized she didn't feel quite as brave as she had a few minutes ago. But she couldn't just sit there. She turned in her seat and took a look through the windows all around the truck before she opened the door, just in case someone was there waiting to jump her. A trio of cars slowly drove by and she found herself closely watching them, heart in her throat, half expecting to see that nutjob from the mesa with his hat pulled down low and a bandanna over the bottom of his face riding inside one of them.

Of course, that was not the case. They were just normal people going about their business in a small western town in Nevada. Nothing threatening about that.

So much for willing herself to be calm and fearless.

Dear Lord, I pray for Your presence and protection and I thank You for it.

Why was prayer so often the last thing she thought of for comfort when it should have been the first?

Pondering that, she crossed the street heading for the accountant's office. Hopefully, talking about numbers would take her thoughts off her other worries for the next hour or so.

Her grandparents and the Sandovals were not wealthy people, but they'd been willing to take a chance and invest their retirement savings in the guest ranch because all of them wanted to live and work in the horse-friendly kind of setting they loved. When they discovered they didn't have enough money to buy the property they'd chosen and pay for all the repairs and renovations they'd need to convert the operation and pay the bills until the business started to turn a profit, Vanessa had contributed her own money to the venture.

And they'd promptly assigned her as the person to deal with the accountant because none of them wanted to do it. But she hadn't minded. A genuine smile crossed her lips as she thought of how blessed she was to have such good and loving people in her life. She would think of them every time the image of that hammer-swinging stalker up on the mesa tried to worm its way back into her mind.

Vanessa had an awkward first few moments with the accountant as she explained the bruises on her face and what had happened to her. Fortunately, after checking to make sure she was all right and didn't need to postpone their discussion, the accountant followed her lead and they quickly redirected the topic to the financial issues concerning the ranch. After an hour and a half of talking numbers, Vanessa was finished and she headed back across the street to the library for the next item on her list of tasks.

This wasn't for the ranch, but for her research into her father's murder. There were many articles about the case, but they yielded frustratingly few details. Vanessa pored over them carefully, hoping to find some detail previously missed or ignored, but her hope dwindled as the hours passed.

Later, when Vanessa stepped out of the library, she gazed out at the dusky horizon to the east. She should have left sooner. But she'd gotten so caught up in old newspapers that she hadn't realized how late it was until a librarian told her they needed to close. She texted Rosa to tell her she was on her way. Rosa replied that she, too, had gotten caught up in what she was learning and had also lost track of time. She would be waiting outside the tech coach's office for Vanessa to pick her up.

Vanessa had printed a few articles at the library and now held the pages in the crook of her arm. Current editions of the *Torchlight Beacon* newspaper were available online, but older editions were not. There were no digitized archives she could access and she'd had to do her research the old-fashioned way by looking at spools of film at the library. At least the clunky old last-millennium viewing machine she'd had to use was connected to a printer.

She started down the steps to the sidewalk and spotted a familiar figure in a dark blue police uniform standing by her grandfather's truck. She glanced around to make sure she hadn't missed a no-parking sign. "Don't tell me you're giving me a ticket," she said to Levi as she walked up to him.

He responded with a half smile and Vanessa's heartbeat sped up a little. Then he shook his head. "No ticket. I just thought I'd hang around until you came out of the library to see how you're doing. And also thank you for sending me the information I'd asked for."

"So you're following me now?" she teased him a little, hoping to see that fleeting bit of a smile again. Most of the time, he looked so serious and professional. Which was fine for a police officer. But that hint of a smile threw something boyish into his appearance. And Vanessa wanted to see it again.

"I didn't have to follow you. I was in the neighborhood." He hooked a thumb toward the police department headquarters on the opposite side of the street the next block down. "The truck you're driving is distinctive. I noticed it when I was at the ranch."

The right front fender of grandpa's truck was canary yellow while the rest of it was sky blue. "I came out to grab something for dinner and spotted it. I went inside the library to see if you were the driver. You looked pretty engrossed in what you were doing. I didn't want to disturb you, and I knew you'd be out soon since it was just about closing time. So, here I am."

He'd been waiting for her. She felt like smiling but didn't let it show.

The tickling sensation in her stomach *had* to be part of the emotional aftereffects from the attack last night. Vanessa Ford did not get giddy over men she barely knew.

"Well, I'm fine," she said, her voice coming out a little higher pitched than normal. "Is there anything else you wanted to talk to me about?"

"Yeah." He held up her phone. "Do you recognize this?"

She nodded and reached for it. "That's mine."

"It was found a pretty good distance from where our trackers believe you tripped." He handed it to her. "I haven't heard back from the phone company about accessing your records yet. If you want to punch in your password and read off the number from the hang-up call you received yesterday, I can send it to our tech guy to trace. Hopefully, it's not an anonymous prepaid number."

She tapped a few digits on the screen until it unlocked. She quickly found the number and read it off. Levi sent his text.

"Is there anything else you need?" she asked.

"That's all for now. But I'm going to hang

around until you're safely back in your truck and on your way."

"Thank you." Vanessa shifted the stack of articles she held in the crook of her arm as she reached into her purse for the truck keys, but she shifted at the wrong angle and the papers fluttered down, fanning across the grimy sidewalk. She snuck a look over to the officer standing by her side. What would be his reaction when he saw that they were all articles about her father's murder?

Levi leaned down to help Vanessa pick up her dropped papers before the breeze sent them out into the street. A slight gust blew one of the sheets over as he reached for it, displaying a screenshot of a front-page banner headline: "Cowboy Shot Dead on Morgan Mesa."

A picture filled the top half of the page and showed a smiling young man wearing a gray cowboy hat and a Western shirt. He had Sam Ford's thick mustache and longish face. But his hair was the same pale blond color as Vanessa's. Below the picture, in smaller type, the caption read "Local rodeo champ Josh Ford dead at twenty-eight."

Vanessa gently tugged at the paper in his hand and he let go of it. Her eyes were red and starting to shimmer. He couldn't imagine what it was like for her to have to read something like that. Never mind the heartache of having to live through it as an eight-year-old child.

"I remember my parents talking about this when it happened," Levi said as he helped her collect the rest of the dropped pages. "They didn't know your dad personally, but they'd seen him competing at Torchlight Rodeo Days a couple of times."

Vanessa straightened the papers in her hands and nodded to let him know she'd heard him. Tears fell from the corners of her eyes and rolled down her face.

Levi took a step forward, about to wrap his arms around her. But then he realized what he was doing and stopped himself. This was a line he did not want to cross. He was a professional, and that was reason enough to hold himself back. He could never acknowledge that spark of personal concern he felt for her. It would only lead to trouble.

Still, he wanted to offer her some comfort. She'd probably just spent at least an hour looking over articles containing awful details and looking at her dad's picture.

There are some experiences you don't ever get over. He knew that from personal experience. He'd seen friends closer than brothers and sisters mortally wounded in combat zones. He still thought of them every single day.

Finally, he reached out and rested his hand on her shoulder. "I'm sorry for your loss." He might have already told her that at the ranch, but he'd tell it to her every day if she needed him to.

"Thank you." She took a deep breath and appeared a little steadier. He let his hand drop back down to his side.

"Nobody was ever brought to trial for what happened to your dad, right?" he asked, trying to remember what had happened in the aftermath. There would be records of the investigation in the police department storage. They would include details that had not been made public.

"No one was charged with the murder," she said. "A few people were brought in for questioning. Two men, Kenny Goren and Eddie Scott, were brought in more than once. People anticipated one or the other would eventually be arrested and charged, but it never happened."

It would be interesting to know if those two men had been cleared of the crime, or if there just wasn't enough evidence to charge them.

While she was talking, Vanessa unlocked the truck and set her papers and purse on the passenger seat.

"I'll follow you back to the ranch," Levi said. "Make sure you get there safely."

"That's not necessary. I won't be going alone. Rosa's in town, too. I'm going to pick her up and we'll ride back to the ranch together."

Levi wasn't convinced that was enough protection.

"Don't worry," Vanessa said as she climbed into the truck. "Rosa brought her gun."

Levi stepped back so she could close the door. Then he watched her start up the truck, cautiously pull away from the curb and then head down the road.

Conducting a murder investigation could be a dangerous undertaking for anyone. Even if the murder was a case that had run cold years ago.

That harrowing attack on the mesa last night might not even be about her dad's murder. But now that Levi had started thinking about her father's case, he couldn't stop. Maybe it was time for the police department to focus on it once again.

Levi walked down the street and into a sandwich shop where he ordered a couple of roast beef subs and two cups of coffee. While he was waiting, he received a text from the police department tech giving the name associated with the hang-up call Vanessa had received. Marv Burke. The name didn't ring any bells for him, but maybe it would mean something to Vanessa.

He carried the food and coffees back to the police station and strode directly to the chief's office, where he knocked on the open door and waited for the chief to stop typing on his keyboard. Finally, Chief Haskell leaned back in his chair and barked out, "Enter."

Levi dropped one of the sandwiches on the desk in front of the chief and set a cup of coffee close to it.

The chief rubbed a thick hand across his freckled bald head and peered suspiciously at Levi. Then he reached for the sandwich. "You obviously want something."

Levi didn't bother trying to deny it. "Chief, do you remember the murder of that cowboy, Josh Ford, up on Morgan Mesa about twenty years ago?"

"Of course." He unwrapped his sandwich. "I was a patrolman back then. Heard the original call go out over the radio after a motorist found the body. You would have just been a kid back then." He popped open the lid on his coffee and took a sip.

"What do you remember about it?"

The chief sighed. "Poor guy was found lying dead in the middle of a road up on the mesa. Single point-blank gunshot to his chest. The newspaper was calling it 'Murder Mesa' for a while. His pickup truck was parked on the edge of the road, the driver's-side door hanging open and the engine still running when he was found."

"What kind of leads did you get?"

"A lot of chatter, but not much physical evidence. There were a couple of suspects that looked good for it, but both got cleared for some reason or other." He shook his head. "It's a shame we were never able to lock anybody up for it. Josh Ford worked on the O'Connell ranch, it was payday and they paid cash, and his wallet was missing. Most of us figured it for a robbery gone bad.

"There were some wild theories about there being a psycho on the loose up there, but on the whole, most people wanted to believe the killer was some transient who was long gone. They get some seasonal workers up there who come and go and nobody ever knows who they really are. Could have been one of them, I suppose."

The chief shrugged and Levi got the feeling he didn't really believe that was the case. "There was also talk that murder might have been the motive and the scene was just set up to look like a robbery. But nobody could ever find anything to prove that."

Levi flipped open the lid on his own coffee and took a sip. "What do you know about Josh Ford?"

When he was a kid, Levi and his family had been fans of the young cowboy. They were all heartbroken when their local hero was murdered, but Levi had been especially devastated. In his young mind it had felt to him like a member of his own family had died. Maybe because each time he'd seen Josh compete, it had been as part of a Hawk family outing. Now, with the perspective of an adult, Levi realized he didn't really know much at all about Vanessa's father.

"I didn't know him personally," the chief said. "Just knew *of* him. He was a good calf roper. Won a lot of competitions. His wife, Claire, was a pretty decent barrel racer. She and her daughter used to dress in matching fancy fringed shirts with lots of rhinestones when they were at a rodeo."

Levi unwrapped his sandwich. "Do you

think it's a coincidence their little girl is the woman who was attacked on the mesa last night? Especially since the attack came after she'd spent the day asking questions about the murder?"

"I feel the same way most cops do about coincidence. It makes me suspect something more is going on." The chief set down his sandwich and wiped the crumbs from his hands. "So you want to reopen the Josh Ford case?" He raised an eyebrow. "In addition to the workload you already have?"

"Yes, sir, I do. Vanessa's questions could be what triggered the attack. She thinks there could be somebody with information who won't talk to a cop, but who will talk to her. And if the attack truly is connected, that means there's information out there someone doesn't want her to find."

The chief took a bite of his sandwich and thought for a moment, then shook his head. "I don't like the idea of a civilian putting herself in danger to do something that's technically police business."

"Yeah, but she seems determined to ask her questions and try to develop some kind of lead. At least if I work with her, I can protect her if she ends up in a dangerous situation."

The chief looked doubtful.

"It's only for a couple of weeks," Levi added. "And then she has to get back to her job in Las Vegas."

"I do like the idea of you keeping an eye on her, especially if there are any additional attacks." The chief leaned back in his chair and crossed his arms over his chest. For a few seconds he turned his gaze away from Levi and toward the window into the squad room where he could watch his officers work. "First the murder, then that stepfather of hers."

"What about the stepfather?" Levi asked. And could he be a suspect for the attack on the mesa?

The chief shifted his gaze back to Levi. "Her mother, Claire Ford, was a young woman when her husband was murdered. She got remarried pretty quickly to Jason Taylor, a regional rodeo star who turned out to have issues with drinking and violence. He moved them out of town, isolated them. Sadly, Claire had to call the cops out to the house a couple of times when he lost his temper and got physical with her. Each time, the same officer responded.

"I don't know what exactly happened. Maybe the stepfather hit the mom and she hit him back. Maybe the stepfather was an excellent liar, or a personal friend of the officer's. In any event, the cop was not correctly trained for domestic violence calls. He told Claire if she pressed charges against her husband, she could be locked up alongside him and possibly lose custody of her daughter. I imagine she didn't know who to turn to for help.

"One night in a drunken rage, Jason fired his gun and nearly hit Vanessa. Her mom grabbed her and ran. She went to the police despite her fears of going to jail and losing her daughter." The chief sighed. "Jason served time. The police officer eventually took a job in another town."

That helped answer a question Levi had been turning over in his mind. Why would a woman whose father had been murdered become a *defense* attorney rather than working for a prosecutor? Maybe it was because her mother could have gotten out of a dangerous situation sooner if she'd gotten some good legal advice.

Life had given Vanessa Ford some hard knocks. But she'd survived them and she was strong. Levi had already seen evidence of that. Still, it wouldn't hurt if she had someone by her side, helping her for a little while. And Levi would like to do exactly that.

"Just don't get tunnel vision," the chief said

and he balled up the paper wrapper from his sandwich and tossed it in the trash. "We've got a modern-day crime to solve with the attack on the mesa last night. The perp you're looking for might try to attack Vanessa again. *That* case is your priority. We don't know for certain if the murder twenty years ago has anything to do with it."

"Yes, sir." Levi's heart ached at the thought of everything Vanessa had already suffered. And there was likely more trouble still to come.

Please, Lord, help me keep her safe.

FOUR

"So the bottom line is Chief Haskell gave me permission to reopen the investigation into your father's murder," Levi said. "And that includes working alongside you and keeping you out of trouble while we question a few people and see if we can drum up any new information." The lieutenant stood on the covered porch of the ranch house.

Vanessa felt such a rush of joy and hope surge through her body when she heard the news that her hands were shaking. After all these years, her dad's cold case was being reopened. The opportunity to find out who murdered her dad was finally here. It was something she'd hoped and prayed for since she was a child, back when the case had first been closed.

"I don't have the words to tell you how truly grateful I am," she said. "I don't think right ones even exist. But thank you."

"I still have other duties to take care of," he said in response, his tone cool and professional. "And that includes searching for the perp who attacked you on the mesa. That means I'll work with you when I can and we have to be efficient with our time."

"Of course," she agreed, anxious to get started.

"And I need your word you won't investigate on your own. I know you said that some people might feel more comfortable talking to you rather than to the police, but you'll need to keep me in the loop, so I can make sure you're safe, even if you're talking to someone privately. We work together on this. I'm authorized to release information to you that hasn't been made public in exchange for your collaboration. But if you go looking around on your own, the deal's off."

"You have my word," she said evenly. Inside, her emotions swirled like a whirlwind. As time had passed with no progress on the murder investigation, especially over the last ten years, she'd grown increasingly afraid that her dad would be forgotten. That the person who murdered him would be able to live a long life with no fear of being captured or serving time for his horrible crime.

"Is there any chance you're free for the next few hours to work on this?" Levi asked.

Actually, she had a lot to do. But none of it mattered as much as finding her dad's killer. "I can work on it now," she said without hesitation.

"Good. I've got an ID on the guy who called you and then hung up. There's always the chance that it was just a misdial. But your phone has a different area code and you'd just spent the day on the mesa asking about your dad. The timing is interesting. Plus, from the information I've seen, it looks like he's lived in this area his whole life. I want to drive up to the mesa and have you talk to him. The chance that he can give us some useful information might be slim, but it's something."

Her heart began to race. This could lead to an actual new lead in the case. "What's his name?"

"Marv Burke. Does the name ring any bells?"

She thought about it for a few seconds and shook her head. "No."

She hurried into the house, quickly grabbed her stuff, told Rosa she was leaving with Levi and headed out the door.

Instead of a marked police SUV, Levi had

driven a pickup truck this time. As they strode over to it, Vanessa glanced over in the direction of the guest cabins where her grandfather and Pablo were working, along with the construction manager and workers they'd hired.

She could tell the exact moment her grandfather spotted her walking with Levi. He stopped sawing the piece of lumber he had propped on a sawhorse and stared in her direction. She waved. He slowly lifted his hand and waved back.

His face was shaded by the brim of his cowboy hat, plus he was a good distance away, but she could guess the expression on his face after seeing his shoulders sag a little. He was worried for her. Maybe even scared.

A quick flare of guilt made her turn away. She didn't want to upset him. But this was something she *had* to do.

Levi opened the passenger door for her, she slid inside and a few seconds later they were heading down the long drive toward the main road.

"So, regarding the investigation into your attack, the volunteer crew we had looking around the Heaton property didn't find any evidence that someone was using the property in any way they shouldn't," Levi said. "So that kills one theory on the motivation for the attack."

"Did they discover anything helpful?"

"Not really. But the Heaton family had their property caretaker come out and take a look at everything. There wasn't any damage to the house other than what you and your attacker did. But a maintenance shed was broken into. That's likely where the hammer came from. Which suggests the attack was not planned very far ahead."

"Did they find the actual hammer?" Vanessa asked. A mental image of it flying past her head flashed through her mind, sending a shiver down her spine. *What might that man have done with the hammer if he'd caught me?*

"They didn't find the hammer. But if it turns up, we'll definitely be able to identify it. All the tools that are kept in that shed have the Heaton name etched into them, so if they're stolen they can't be pawned. Not by a reputable pawnbroker, anyway."

They were on a steep section of road heading up the mesa. The towering pines were spread a little sparser, revealing glimpses of blue sky and snow-tipped mountain peaks in the distance. The area around Torchlight and Morgan Mesa was beautiful, but also heartbreaking for

Vanessa. Whenever she came back for a visit, she couldn't help thinking of her dad and what it would have been like if he were still alive.

"What do you know about this man we're going to see, Marv Burke?" She turned to Levi. "Have you talked to him?"

"I haven't. I'm going to let you have first crack at that. I know he's about your dad's age, maybe a couple of years younger. He has a few minor drug possession charges on his record from around the time of the murder, but nothing since then. And he owns the Mustang Express gas station and convenience store." Levi glanced over at her. "One of the places where you stopped to talk to people. It was listed on the timeline you sent me."

He pulled over onto a dirt turnout, then searched for a copy of Marv Burke's driver's license picture on his phone and showed it to Vanessa.

The guy looked like he was in his midforties, clean-shaven and tanned, with dark blond hair that appeared to be pulled back in a ponytail.

"Could he be the guy with the hammer?" Levi asked.

She stared at the picture. "I can't tell," she finally said. "His face was covered and he wore a hat. But his height and weight fit the size of the guy who attacked me."

She handed the phone back to Levi. "I remember talking to a woman at the cash register when I stopped there. I gave her my contact information and told her I'd be in the area for most of the day, and that I'd be on the Heaton property around sunset to walk around a bit like I did with my dad when I was little. I think I mentioned that to everybody I talked to."

Levi cut a sideways glance at her and made a sound of frustration as he pulled back onto the road.

"I know," Vanessa said, shaking her head. "In hindsight, I can see how stupid that was. But I was hoping to gain some sympathy. I thought maybe adding that touch of emotion would cause someone to open up who otherwise might not say anything. And who knows?" she said, as the Mustang Express came into view just up ahead. "Maybe it worked."

"When we walk in, I want you to take the lead," Levi said as he pulled into a parking space. "If Marv isn't working the register, ask for him. I'll hang back."

She glanced at him. "You realize, even in civilian clothes, it's pretty obvious you're a cop."

"He won't know for certain unless I have to flash my badge."

The Mustang Express convenience store looked a little weathered on the outside, but inside it had lots of gleaming clean metallic surfaces. Vanessa walked up to the clerk at the register and asked for Marv. The clerk called out to the back office area to summon him.

When Marv walked out and saw Vanessa, his eyes widened. Then his glance shifted to Levi and lingered on him, before returning to Vanessa. "How may I help you?"

Vanessa introduced herself and then said, "You called me yesterday. I'd like to know why."

Marv crossed his arms and shook his head. "I didn't call you."

"Yes, you did." She took out her phone and showed him the screen with his number on it. "I'm grateful that you called," she said, softening her tone. "Because I believe you were going to tell me something important about my dad."

Marv sighed. "I heard about what happened to you at the Heaton place and I'm sorry. That's all I have to say about that." He glanced again at Levi. "Are you a cop?" he asked.

Levi didn't respond.

"If you think I had anything to do with it—"

"I just want to know why you called me," Vanessa quickly interjected. "And why you hung up."

Marv glanced at the clerk, who was obviously trying to listen in. "Let's talk outside."

"I hung up because I had second thoughts about saying anything," Marv said once they were standing in the bright sunlight with a brisk, cool breeze blowing across the mesa. "All of that happened a long time ago. And maybe it's smarter for me not to get involved."

"*How* are you involved?" Vanessa asked. Beside her, she could almost feel the effort it took for Levi to stay quiet and not join the conversation.

"I'm not involved," Marv said. "I just saw something the night your father was shot and killed. Maybe it's related, maybe not."

Vanessa swallowed thickly, not certain if she was going to want to hear the answer to her question. "What did you see?"

"Two men fighting by the side of the road."

"Was one of them my dad?"

Marv shook his head. "Couldn't have been. This was after his time of death. I was working at a filling station back then. We had an old TV in the office and there was a newsflash about someone finding his body. The road where it happened was blocked while the cops investigated and that was the route I normally took to drive home. When I got off work that night, I took a different unpaved road home. I came across two guys slugging it out and I remember thinking, 'Man, what a weird night.'"

"Did you recognize either of the men?" Levi asked.

Marv turned to him. "Nah. I thought about telling the police, but then I figured it likely wasn't related. Probably just a couple of drunk fools fighting on a Friday night." He sighed deeply. "The cops and I weren't exactly on good terms back then. I was young and stupid. I thought about it a couple of times over the years, though. When you came in and I overheard you talking to Amy at the register, I thought, 'I'll call her and finally get this off my chest.' But when you answered the phone, I hesitated and I hung up."

"Will you show us where you saw that fight?" Levi asked.

Marv shrugged. "Sure, why not?" They agreed that they'd follow him, and watched from their truck as he got into a shiny black muscle car parked on the edge of the lot and led the way onto a bumpy dirt road until he finally stopped at a spot with a cluster of trees and a fenced field just beyond them.

After they got out of their vehicles, Marv waved toward the area where he thought he'd seen the fight. "Best I can remember, it was right about here."

"Is this Heaton property or O'Connell property?" Vanessa asked.

Marv rubbed his hand over his chin. "I'm not sure. This is right about where the property lines meet."

"Have you told anybody else about this?" Levi asked.

"I've mentioned it to a couple of people over the years." He indicated Vanessa. "After she came by the other day, I told my employees about it. Speaking of which, I need to get back to work."

Vanessa and Levi thanked him for his help. He got back into his car and gunned it down the road.

Levi walked around, kicking at the dirt and grass with the toe of his cowboy boot.

"Do you think there could still be evidence here after all this time?" Vanessa asked him.

"Like Marv said, what he saw could have just been a couple of random fools out here fighting. Whoever they were, they might not have left anything behind. And if they did, the evidence could have blown away or disintegrated by now. But it's worth looking. We've got a really good volunteer group that would love to get up here and search around. They found your phone. Maybe they'll find something up here."

"Could Marv be the guy with the hammer?" Levi asked as they got back into his truck.

Vanessa slowly shook her head. "I just don't know."

"Once Marv said something to his employees about that fight he'd seen all those years ago, the story likely spread like wildfire in this little community," Levi said. "You said you stopped at the Mustang Express about eight in the morning. The attack was at about five that same evening. Plenty of time for word to get back to your attacker, if it wasn't Marv himself."

Vanessa felt a chill and rubbed her hands over her arms. "I don't understand why his story about a fight would lead to an attack on me. And if there was some kind of evidence up here, wouldn't someone have taken it away years ago?"

"Somebody might be worried they left some

kind of clue up here. Maybe they were afraid you'd come up here, look around and you'd find it."

"I know it's been a long afternoon for you, but do you feel like stopping by the O'Connell ranch?" Levi was looking at the screen on his phone, where he'd opened the timeline Vanessa had sent him. They were sitting in his truck in a parking lot after taking a break to get coffee and bear claws.

"I'd like to do as much as we can today," Vanessa said. "I've got a couple of appointments tomorrow. And in the evening, the City Commerce Committee is having their quarterly meeting at the Fargo Hotel. I plan to be there. Networking is going to be an important part of making the guest ranch business a success. Rosa and Pablo have offered to help out with that, but they're a little nervous about getting started. Before the attack on the mesa they asked me to go with them to their first meeting and I promised them I would."

Levi felt uneasy about that. "Let me check my schedule to see if I can escort you."

"Don't worry. Rosa has already told me she'll be armed. Just in case." Vanessa pulled a pair of sunglasses out of her handbag and slipped them on. The corners were studded with rhinestones and the light glinting off them was practically blinding. “Grandpa isn’t very social and wants no part of it.”

They’d managed to stop at every place on Vanessa’s list except for the O’Connell ranch. Fortunately, people at the various businesses had been cooperative and Levi was able to compile a long list of employees who’d been working when Vanessa originally stopped by. One of them could be her attacker. Checking out everyone on the list would be tedious work, but big crimes were often solved by small details.

“I appreciate all the time you’re putting into this,” Vanessa said.

Levi nodded, but instead of looking at her, he watched a car drive by them in the parking lot. Sometimes, when he looked into Vanessa’s eyes for too long, he felt like he was being drawn in. Like he was starting to feel a connection to her. And that could not happen. He wouldn’t let it. He’d promised himself he would focus on work and helping other people. And that meant a romantic relationship was out of the question.

"I'm just doing my job," he said, keeping his tone professional and distant.

She took a sip of coffee. "People assume because I'm a defense attorney I don't like cops. Especially when they see me cross-examine them in court. But that isn't true at all," she said, not sounding the slightest bit put off. "I believe in the work you do. My only goal is to get to the truth, and sometimes that means asking hard questions. The fact is, everybody makes mistakes. Even cops."

"Agreed. We're all human. You don't always do somebody a favor when you call them heroic and act as if they can do no wrong," Levi said. "Sometimes that makes their job harder."

"Somebody called you *heroic* and you didn't like it?"

Levi nodded. "When I came home after serving in the Marine Corps, people called me a hero. I wasn't one. I saw combat. I did my job. That was it. There were people who deserved to be called heroes. But not me. Sometimes they start to talk a similar way about me doing my job as a cop. I don't like it."

He turned the key in the ignition and the truck rumbled to life. He pulled the truck out onto the road so he'd have an excuse not to look in her eye as he said the next part—the part she deserved to know before she put too much trust in him. "When I got back stateside, I lived in California for a little over a year. I drank *a lot.* I acted like an idiot *a lot.*" He blew out a deep sigh. "I have a sister, Angela. Two years older than me. We've always been close, had each other's backs.

"When I was in California, indulging myself in stupidity, her husband walked out on her without warning. She was living in Texas. Had three sons, the youngest was still a baby. She called me asking for help. With money and moving. Wanting some emotional support. And I totally blew her off. I wasn't there for her at all."

Levi slipped on his sunglasses. They didn't have bling like hers did, but the lenses were very dark, and he felt the need for something to hide behind. He was still so ashamed when he thought of his behavior back then. Once he'd pulled himself together, he rededicated his life to helping others rather than focusing on himself. It had led to conflicts with some women he dated who complained when the job came first, but in the end, he couldn't regret it.

"I imagine you were going through some pretty tough times of your own," Vanessa said.

She was trying to be kind and Levi appreciated that. But he let the conversation drop. He didn't want to have to pretend to be a hero. The only way he could live with himself was by acknowledging that he *wasn't* one.

"So, you didn't talk to Robert O'Connell when you originally came by here, right?" Levi asked as he made the turn onto the ranch property. Robert was a fourth-generation rancher. Levi didn't know him personally, but he had a high profile in the community. His son, Trent, was already starting to take over the enterprise.

"I spoke with a couple of ranch hands," Vanessa answered. "One of them told me Robert was off the property and wasn't due back until evening. And that Trent was out of town."

This time Robert was at home. "Vanessa Ford, I haven't seen you in a very long time," he said with a broad smile as he ushered them into a large wood-paneled den.

Levi reckoned Robert to be about Sam Ford's age, with a horseshoe-shaped ring of graying blond hair around his otherwise bald head. And like Vanessa's grandpa, he had the physique of an older gentleman who still did physical labor.

"Mr. O'Connell used to come around our house and help my mom out after my dad was gone," Vanessa said to Levi after the introductions were made.

Levi considered that bit of information. Sometimes someone helped out after a crime because they were kind. Sometimes it was because they were involved in the crime and felt guilty about it.

"I heard about what happened to you on the Heaton property." Robert shook his head. "I was as sorry as I could be to hear about it." He glanced at Levi. "You look familiar. You're a police officer, correct?"

"Yes, sir."

"I came by to talk to you not long before it happened," Vanessa said to Robert. "I left my phone number. The ranch hand I spoke to, he said his name was Darryl, said he'd tell you."

"I'm sorry, honey. I didn't get the message. Darryl is just out of his teens. He's a hard worker, but not exactly focused. Except when it comes to horses." He gestured toward a leather-covered couch and matching chairs and they all sat down.

"I'd wanted to ask what you remembered about the night my dad was murdered."

Robert rubbed his hands on his thighs. "That was a long time ago and I've forgotten a lot of the details. But at the time I told the police everything I knew. Which wasn't much. What are you asking now?"

"Did you ever hear any rumors or speculation about what happened?" Levi asked. "Maybe someone had a theory of who might have been involved?"

"Just the same things everybody else heard. That Kenny Goren was the killer but somehow got away with it. The cops brought him down to the station several times. It was in the papers."

Levi moved Kenny Goren to the top of his mental suspect list. He wanted to know what evidence had kept him from being charged with the crime.

"Where were you when the murder happened?" Levi asked.

"Home. Exhausted. It was a busy time of year. I was sitting on the couch in front of the TV, half asleep, when the show was interrupted by a news announcement that his body had been found."

"Where were you when Vanessa was attacked at the Heaton House?"

"I don't know exactly what time that happened." Robert arched a graying eyebrow but kept his voice calm. "I was in town from noon until about two having lunch with a couple of members of the City Commerce Committee. We're having a meeting tomorrow night at the

Fargo Hotel. After that I ran a few errands and then came home."

"I'll be at that meeting tomorrow night," Vanessa said.

Robert smiled at her. "I've heard about the impending launch of the Silver Horse Guest Ranch. I think it's a great idea. How are your grandpa and the Sandovals doing?"

Levi watched Robert O'Connell closely while Robert and Vanessa chatted about what each of them had been doing over the last few years. Robert never did mention what he'd been doing during the time of the attack on Vanessa.

"Where's Trent?" Vanessa asked Robert just before they left.

"He's been out of town for a few days. He negotiates most of our business contracts now. Buying the supplies we need and selling the animals we raise. It keeps him busy."

"Is that him?" Levi pointed to a picture on the wall as they walked out toward the front door. A cowboy in his late thirties, about ten years younger than the age Vanessa's dad would have been, stood proudly beside a dark-haired woman and a couple of adolescent boys at what looked like a rodeo.

"That's him." A hint of sadness flickered across Robert's face. "His wife and my grandsons live in Lake Tahoe these days." After that, they said their goodbyes and headed out to the truck.

Levi walked beside Vanessa and opened the door for her. "What do you think?" he asked, when they were inside the truck and he was certain Robert O'Connell couldn't hear them. "Could he be the man who attacked you on the mesa?"

Vanessa sat back in the seat and her shoulders slumped. "I have good childhood memories of Mr. O'Connell. I don't want to believe it was him."

"And yet?"

"He is the same size as the guy with the hammer. And my attacker disguised his voice, which makes me wonder if he thought I'd recognize it." She sighed deeply and shook her head. "Right now, I don't know what to think."

"When they're finished refurbishing this place, it's going to look beautiful," Rosa said, glancing around at the interior of the Fargo Hotel the following evening.

"It has such great history," Pablo added. "Can't you just see the old cowboys with their spurs and the ladies with their long dresses and fancy hats walking through here?"

Vanessa could easily imagine what Pablo described. The hotel had been built back in the 1880s, right next to the old train depot. The old depot had been torn down and the modern railroad lines had been rerouted years ago, but the hotel had stayed. It had been expanded and remodeled many times over the years, and it was being renovated again right now.

Remodel work had stopped for the day and several people passed through the lobby heading for the Commerce Committee meeting being held in a small banquet room.

"I wish Grandpa had come," Vanessa said as they strode across the thick maroon carpet. "It would be good for him to get out and see people."

Pablo chuckled. "Like he told you just before we left, he'll see plenty of people when they come to stay at the ranch."

"Yeah, but the guest ranch won't get many repeat customers if the people who run it aren't friendly."

"Oh, Sam is plenty friendly when he's on his own turf," Rosa said and gave Vanessa's arm a quick, reassuring squeeze.

Vanessa glanced around as she walked and caught sight of herself in a mirror. The makeup she'd put on didn't completely conceal the bruises on her cheek and chin. Not exactly the first impression she wanted to make at this meeting, showing up bruised and battered. But at least she was here.

After all Vanessa had been through that was something.

In the next moment her thoughts drifted back to the attack on the mesa and a fist of terror punched her in the solar plexus, stopping her in her tracks. A flashback to the attack at Heaton House took over her thoughts, quickly followed by an image of her father, dead on the highway. Her blood felt chilled in her veins and her teeth began to chatter.

What was happening? It felt as if the emotions she'd been fighting so hard to keep under control had burst through a dam.

Now? Did it have to happen *now*?

But there was nothing she could do to stop it. The person who had murdered her father had never been caught. Maybe she'd come face-to-face with that killer up on the mesa. Maybe he hadn't just meant to scare her. Maybe she'd be dead now if Levi hadn't shown up when he had.

And maybe he was close by, even now. How would she know?

"Honey, are you okay?" Rosa placed both her hands on Vanessa's shoulders.

"You want to go back home?" Pablo asked, concern keeping his voice low and gentle. "We can turn around and go back to the ranch right now. Who wants to go to some boring business meeting, anyway?"

"No, I'm fine." From the corner of her eye, Vanessa saw the mayor and the Commerce Committee vice-president walk past.

She drew in a deep breath. Squared her shoulders. Tried to smile even though her entire body was trembling.

She *had* to pull herself together. Rosa, Pablo and Vanessa's grandfather had all put their life savings into the Silver Horse Guest Ranch. Coming to this meeting tonight wasn't about Vanessa, it was about them and their financial future.

She drew in another deep breath and reminded herself that she was surrounded by plenty of people in a public place. She would not allow that man from the mesa to get into her thoughts and control her through terror. She would go to this meeting. And she was going to make good use of her time here.

"I'm all right," she said with an apologetic

glance at Rosa and Pablo. "Just let me touch up my makeup."

Rosa went with her. The main ladies' room in the lobby had a temporarily closed sign on the door and scaffolding in front of it, so they threaded their way down a hall that ran by the hotel's restaurant until they found their way to a smaller ladies' room where Vanessa could silently give herself a pep talk and more thoroughly cover up the bruises.

By the time they met Pablo back in the lobby, Vanessa had warmed up and managed to shift her thoughts mostly back to their business plans.

"All those years without seeing you, and now I see you twice in two days," Robert O'Connell said, stepping up to her seemingly from out of nowhere and smiling. "I'm a fortunate man." His gaze shifted to Pablo and he stuck out his hand. "Pablo, it's been a long time." They shook hands. And then he greeted Rosa and shook hands with her.

"It's great to see all of you," Robert said to them. "And with your permission, I'd like to introduce all three of you to the people in Torchlight who want to keep our local economy growing." He walked beside them into the meeting room.

An hour and a half later, the meeting was over.

While Rosa and Pablo chatted with some people they'd just met, Vanessa walked over to a side table and picked up a vanilla cupcake she'd been eyeing for a while. It was delicious, but messy.

When she was finished with it, she headed out toward the ladies' room to wash frosting off her hands, her mind filled with thoughts of the ranch and opportunities she'd just learned about. There were possibilities for their guest ranch to work with other businesspeople and planned events like the city Easter egg hunt in the park and the Christmas parade. All events that could draw people to Torchlight and help generate revenue for the ranch.

She made the turn in the lobby and headed down the hallway. After a few steps, she could hear someone walking behind her. Probably Rosa. She started to turn her head, and then everything went black.

FIVE

Levi sat at his desk, tapping the computer keys and finishing a report at the end of a long day, when a supervisor stepped through the passage from the communications room and called out to him. "Vanessa Ford's been assaulted."

"Dispatch EMS," Levi snapped as he jumped to his feet.

"We've already taken care of that," the supervisor responded.

Levi pulled on his jacket. "Where is she?"

"Fargo Hotel."

He reached for his phone. "I'm heading over there."

A sickening wave of fear and regret turned Levi's stomach as he strode through the office and out the door. He should have assigned a patrol officer to go to that meeting with her. *He* should have gone himself to protect her. But there'd been no further threat since the initial attack. There was unfinished business from his other cases he needed to take care of. He'd talked the situation over with the chief and they'd decided the public setting and the people accompanying Vanessa would be enough to deter anyone from harming her.

Wrong.

The hotel was close by and he considered running there. But there was the grim possibility that he might need to drive her to the hospital if she was in bad shape and he got there before the ambulance arrived.

He got into his police SUV and raced the short distance to the hotel.

"What happened?" he impatiently demanded of the hotel security employee who was waiting outside the hotel entrance as Levi got out of the SUV.

"Ms. Ford was knocked unconscious and dragged into a service area and left there. One of our employees found her."

Levi could hear the wail of an ambulance getting closer to the hotel. Once inside, his gaze swept across the lobby, taking in the cloth-draped scaffolding and construction supplies. There could still be a potential assailant hiding in the shadows. He'd be no help to Vanessa if the scene weren't secure.

Levi turned to the hotel security employee. “Where is she?”

“We’ve got her in a safe location where she’s being guarded. Follow me.”

Emergency medical workers pushed a gurney through the front door. Two patrol officers walked briskly alongside them.

Levi directed the officers to stay in the lobby. Most of the potential witnesses to the attack had probably already left. Still, he gave the order, “Nobody in or out.” Then he turned his attention back to the hotel security employee.

“We have Ms. Ford in the employee lounge,” the man said. “Behind the main desk. This way.”

Levi followed, with the emergency medical responders right behind them. Combat experience had taught Levi to keep his head on a swivel. As he looked around, he noticed the hotel restaurant and across from it a small gift shop. Both were closed for the remodeling project and both were places where the attacker could be hiding.

Inside the employee lounge, Vanessa sat in a chair while Rosa pressed a cloth to the side of her head. Pablo stood behind Vanessa, softly patting her shoulder as if she were a child.

The tight grip that had squeezed Levi’s heart

from the moment he'd first heard the news of the assault eased a little. Vanessa was conscious, alert, looking around. That was a relief. Still, dark red speckles of blood fanned across the platinum-blond curls on the left side of her head and the left shoulder of her pale blue sparkling blouse. Once again, he found himself thinking of the photo of the little girl in the fancy rodeo outfit who'd just lost her father in a horrible way. Hadn't she been through enough?

His jaw tightened as he came to a now inescapable conclusion. The attacker on the mesa *had* targeted her personally. She wasn't simply in the wrong place at the wrong time up on the mesa. If he'd needed any proof, this was it.

So, was the attacker tonight the same person? Whoever it was, they had to be desperate to launch an assault this brazen. And quite likely it was someone local if they knew the Fargo was a good place for a stealthy attack with its winding old hallways and general chaos because of the remodel.

And what was their goal? If they'd meant to kill Vanessa, they could have done that while she was unconscious. It looked like another attempt to scare her.

"How are you?" he asked Vanessa softly,

pulling up a chair beside her so they could talk while the paramedic took her vital signs.

She turned to look directly at him, and her dark blue eyes were so filled with fear and pain that he felt like he'd been punched. From the time he'd met her, he'd watched her battle fear using humor and a seemingly natural confidence. But right now, fear was winning. She'd been robbed of the strength she'd fought so hard to sustain. Her assailant had stolen it from her. Levi wanted very much to find the jerk and make him pay.

In between answering the paramedic's questions as she looked into Vanessa's eyes with a penlight and then took her pulse, Vanessa told Levi what had happened. It wasn't much of a story and she offered no useful details. She'd gone to wash her hands in the ladies' room and been blindsided.

"Did you see anyone here tonight or maybe hear a voice that reminded you of the attacker on the mesa?" Levi asked.

"No." She sucked in her breath as the paramedic began to feel around Vanessa's new injury.

"Did you notice anybody watching you closely?" Levi continued questioning Vanessa.

"No."

He turned to Rosa and Pablo. "Did either of you notice anything?"

Looking miserable, they both sadly shook their heads.

The hotel security chief walked into the room with an electronic tablet. "I've got surveillance footage for you, Lieutenant Hawk. It's queued up and ready to go." He handed the tablet to Levi.

After watching all of the available footage, it was clear none of the cameras were angled directly toward the area where Vanessa had been attacked. Levi could see Vanessa walking through a couple of different sections of the lobby. He could also see four men and three women walking through at about the same time. But there were no clear images of faces. In some spots, there was scaffolding in the way. In others, the security cameras had probably been bumped out of alignment as the remodeling work was being done.

There was no view at all of the short hallway leading to the ladies' room where the attack had happened.

The paramedic finished with her examination and recommended Vanessa go to the hospital just to make certain she was all right.

"See, even an expert thinks you need to get

your head examined," Pablo joked feebly. Rosa elbowed him in the side.

Vanessa frowned. "I'm all right."

Levi recognized the familiar stubborn look on Vanessa's face. In a sense, that was a good thing. It could mean the terror of getting attacked for a second time was subsiding and she was getting some of her strength and confidence back.

But it also meant it would be that much harder to get her to go to the hospital when she didn't want to go.

Fortunately, this time he had a little leverage. He pulled up a chair and sat down next to her. "I think you should go get checked out."

"I just want to go back to the ranch and crawl into bed," she said.

He hesitated, then took her hand, small and cool, and held it between his. "You've been through a lot already. Having this second injury so close to the first could lead to problems if you don't take care of it properly."

They sat with their gazes locked for a few seconds. Then her cheeks turned pink and she looked away. Probably due to the headache he'd heard her mention to the paramedic.

She pulled her hand from his and cleared her throat. "I can take care of myself."

"I have no doubt of that." He leaned back and pulled his phone out of his pocket. "But if you don't go to the hospital and get checked out, I'll call your grandfather."

She pursed her lips and glared at him. The look of fire in her eyes made him feel much more confident about a good prognosis. Still, he kept the pressure on her and held up the phone screen so she could see her grandfather's name on his contact list. "I'm not bluffing. Come on. I'll go with you."

She rolled her eyes, then got unsteadily to her feet. Levi wrapped his hand around her arm so he could hold her if she started to fall. She waved off the EMT trying to direct her toward the gurney and started walking. "All right. Let's go to the hospital."

"Tell me, honey, are you waiting for somebody to knock your head clean off your body before you'll stop this investigation?" Sam Ford drew himself up to his full height, looking as tough and unbending as a railroad spike, and stared down into Vanessa's eyes. "What's it gonna take for you to head back to Las Vegas where I hope you'll be safe?" He made a derisive snorting sound and shook his head, muttering, "Never thought I'd think of Vegas as being safe."

Vanessa knew "tough love" didn't come easy to her grandfather. If he was riding herd on a cluster of cowboys acting like fools, he had no problem telling them his exact opinion of their behavior and knocking a few heads together. But when he was disciplining Vanessa, she could always see the pain and guilt in his eyes. Even now, while he stubbornly held her gaze, she could tell by the way he chewed his bottom lip that he already regretted yelling at her.

She loved him every bit as much as he loved her. Even when he was trying to pick a fight. So she gave him the best smile she could muster.

His shoulders slumped. He looked down and kicked the pointed toe of his cowboy boot into the dirt.

They were outside in the afternoon sunlight, standing by the small corral close to the house. Farther out, in the larger corral at the other end of the stables, Pablo worked with several horses that had just been delivered to the ranch very early this morning.

Vanessa had been feeding a few carrots to her grandparents' beloved old horse, Maybelle, when her grandfather had stormed out of the house.

She'd gone to the hospital last night and been released after a couple of hours when the doctor found no evidence of a serious injury. He'd advised over-the-counter pain medication and listed several warning signs to watch for. Levi made a point of explaining those warning signs to Sam when he'd brought her home. The sorrowful expression on her grandpa's face when she walked through the door had nearly broken Vanessa's heart. She'd been afraid if she spoke, she'd burst into tears.

Sam had asked her to let go of the investigation and hand it all over to the police. He'd reminded her that even if they found out who murdered her father, it wouldn't bring him back. Her drive for justice wasn't worth the risk. When Levi called this morning to check on her she told him about her grandfather's request.

He assured her the Torchlight Police Department was one hundred percent committed to reopening the investigation whether she was in town or not. Marv's story of the fight by the side of the road was a new lead to pursue. And though no physical evidence had been found in the area, something could still turn up. The citizen volunteers who were helping with the search were supposed to get back to work this morning at first light. They had continually expanded the perimeter of the search area in case Marv's memory of the location was off.

After wrestling with her decision for several hours over whether she should stay and continue to try and find her father's killer or go back to Vegas, Vanessa had finally made up her mind and told her grandfather about her decision to stay and continue investigating. Apparently, he'd bitten his tongue for as long as he could before stomping out here and telling her what he thought about it.

Vanessa turned her attention back to Maybelle and leaned over the corral fence to give the graying mare a couple more good scratches on the white blaze marking on her forehead. Maybelle was officially retired and nobody rode her anymore, but she'd always been a good listener. Vanessa had been talking to her before her grandpa had stormed up.

Of course, Vanessa was afraid to stay in Torchlight. She was terrified, in fact. But she didn't know who was after her and there was no guarantee if she went home to Vegas that the assailant wouldn't follow her there.

She glanced over at her grandfather. His

gaze was fixed in the direction of the mesa that loomed over the town.

Somedays it seemed like nothing was simple and no decisions were easy.

Maybelle tossed her head back a couple of times to get Vanessa's attention and chuffed impatiently. The horse wanted more carrots. They were all out of them, but there were apples in a basket on the kitchen counter.

The rumbling sound of an engine drew Vanessa's attention to a police department pickup truck heading up the long drive.

"That's Levi," she said. "He called a short time ago and told me he was coming out here." She waved in the direction of the vehicle. It continued on, following the driveway until it was blocked from view by the house. Shortly after that, Levi strode into view and exchanged greetings with Vanessa and her grandfather.

"Looks like you're adding some nice stock to the place," Levi said, gesturing toward Pablo and the recently arrived horses.

Vanessa nodded. Her grandfather needed to get over there and help Pablo. Working the horses would help him calm down and lift his spirits.

"The horses are from a resort in Arizona near Scottsdale," Vanessa explained to Levi.

"The owners of the property decided to change a few things around and the horses had to go. They're a little older and not used to doing much more than following one another on a well-known trail, which makes them perfect for our future guests. When Grandpa first contacted the wrangler, he was so relieved to have a potential buyer for the lot of them that he practically gave them away."

"I'm glad things worked out for the horses."

"Do you ride?" she asked.

He nodded. "Grew up on a ranch. My parents raised cattle. My sister runs it now. The Twin Pines Ranch."

"Oh, that's east of town in the foothills." Vanessa was a little surprised. How could she have spent this much time around him and not already know that? But now that she thought about it, the Hawk family name in connection with that ranch did seem familiar. "Did you join the Marines because you didn't like ranching?"

He shook his head. "I like ranching. I became a Marine because my dad and my grandfather served in the military. I admired that, and wanted to do it, too. I never intended for it to be a career. I actually thought I'd come home and work the ranch after I got out. But by then my sister was divorced, had moved back home, and she was running it. And doing a very good job. The problem is, it's not that big of a ranch. It brings in enough money to take care of my parents, my sister and her sons, and that's about it. But it's all right. I like being a cop, too."

"Any chance you came out here to talk some sense into my granddaughter?" Sam grumbled. "Get her to stop asking questions about what happened to her dad and just let it rest?"

Vanessa sighed. So much for thinking her grandpa was coming to terms with her decision.

"No, sir." Levi took off the cowboy hat that was standard-issue for the Torchlight Police Department and held it alongside his body. "I have some news that I wanted to tell the two of you in person." He drew in a breath and let his gaze settle on Vanessa. "We just found your dad's wallet near the road about a half-mile west of where Marv said he saw the two men fighting."

Hearing the news created a ripple of goose bumps across Vanessa's skin and a sad mixture of emotions slowly tumbled through her heart. She was relieved to have a new tangible clue in the case after all these years. But it was also unbearably sad to be reminded that her father was murdered for the seven hundred dollars he'd had in his wallet that payday Friday night.

She turned her gaze from Levi's dark brown eyes, filled with compassion, and looked to her grandpa. Sam's shoulders slumped, almost as though he'd just taken a punch in his chest. But then he straightened his spine. The expression in his eyes was hard and glassy.

"Did you bring the wallet with you?" Vanessa asked, uncertain if she could touch it or even see it without bursting into tears.

"It's down at the police station. Forensics is going over it, just in case there's a trace of anything that could help."

"Like a fingerprint?" Sam asked.

Levi tapped his cowboy hat against the side of his leg. "I'd caution you against getting your hopes up about finding any evidence like that. The wallet's very weathered. It was found in pieces. A small metal horseshoe that was apparently on the front of the wallet set off a handheld metal detector."

Sam pursed his lips together. "That's Josh's wallet, all right. Bought it at a rodeo near Carson City."

"His driver's license and a couple of credit cards were found with it."

Sam stepped over to Vanessa, wrapped his arms around her and squeezed her tight. His embrace gave her that same feeling of comfort it always had. But it couldn't erase the heartache that had never completely gone away since she'd heard the horrible news about her dad back when she was eight years old.

"Honey, I don't want whoever did this to your dad to come after you," Sam said, still holding her tight. His voice had softened to a point where she thought it might break, which was so much worse than hearing him snarl. Finally, he let her go. But she got the feeling he didn't really want to.

"Grandpa, the police were able to find dad's wallet because someone who wasn't willing to talk to the police twenty years ago was willing to talk to me when I came by and asked. Maybe that will happen again." She took a shaky breath. "And I can't let somebody bully me without at least trying to fight back. Not again." She was speaking in statements, but she could hear the pleading tone in her own voice.

Sam looked at her and let his head tilt just a little. As if he'd just been defeated. They both knew she was referring to her stepfather.

Vanessa turned to Levi. She wasn't a person who was comfortable sharing details of her private life. But the person who'd attacked her twice now *had* to be caught. The monster who'd murdered her dad couldn't be allowed to get away with what he'd done. She was determined to tell Levi about every single person she could think of who might be capable of killing her dad. She couldn't stand the thought of the investigation reaching a dead end and remaining unsolved forever. That meant she had to be willing to tell Levi some pretty sensitive details of her life if it would help catch a criminal and bring her and her grandfather some measure of peace.

"My former stepfather, Jason, was a bully," she started out. "He liked to fight and push people around."

"If your grandmother and I had had any idea of what he was doing—"

"I know," Vanessa said gently. Grandpa had told her many times before that if he'd known about her stepfather's explosive temper he would have come and gotten her and taken her home to live with him and Grandma. And she believed him. Eventually, her grandparents did take custody of her.

"My mom was a barrel racer when she was young," Vanessa continued. "She loved to dress for competitions in fringe and rhinestones with her hair curled and piled atop her head. She'd dress me up the same way, and my dad would grin and carry on about how he had the most beautiful girls in the world."

Levi watched her closely but didn't interrupt.

"Mom was young and scared after we lost Dad and she remarried quickly. A cowboy at the end of his rodeo career who drank too much. He moved us eighty miles away to Walker Valley where we didn't know anybody. As his career was tanking and he was getting more and more depressed, it made him angry to see my mom happy. He demanded that she stop wearing the flashy cowgirl clothes she liked. Stop drawing attention to herself."

Vanessa could see Levi's jaw muscle tighten.

Sam looked off into the distance, like there was something important he needed to study at the edge of the tree line. Vanessa knew hearing her talk about that time in her childhood was still upsetting for him. Even after all these years.

"I've heard a little bit about your former stepfather," Levi said. "The police chief told me how the story ended."

Vanessa was grateful she didn't have to go into more detail. "My mom remarried quickly yet again after that, but her current husband is okay. They moved to Arizona. I moved in with my grandparents."

"I'll check out this Jason guy," Levi said in a flat tone. "See if he's still in town and if he holds some kind of grudge against you."

Could that really have been Jason up on the mesa? Wouldn't she have recognized him? And yet, the man had tried to disguise his voice...

Maybelle, who'd been waiting patiently in the corral for more treats, tossed her head and snorted. Vanessa reached over the rail to scratch the horse's head a little bit more.

"Now that we've found your dad's wallet, Chief Haskell and I were thinking you might want to talk to the media," Levi said. "Specifically to the senior reporter from the *Torchlight Beacon*. They have a reasonably sized readership. The attacks on you have already made it into the news and I hope that might generate some leads. But what I'm talking about right now would be an interview with you, where you could remind people of your dad's case and mention the fight by the side of the road. Since traffic was rerouted for several hours that night while the police investigated Josh's murder, it's possible somebody else drove past that same spot and saw the fight. Perhaps they could identify one or both people. Or maybe they saw something else and never reported it because they had no reason to think it was connected to the murder."

Vanessa nodded. "I'll do it."

Sam had been quietly listening for a while. Now he crossed his arms over his chest and frowned at Vanessa. Afraid of what he might say, she felt her heart rise up in her throat.

"If you want to stay in town and make sure justice is served or whatever it is you're doing, I won't try to stop you," Sam said. "But don't you do anything foolish. It isn't just your life that's in danger. My life is in danger, too. Because *you* are my life, little girl."

Tears burned in Vanessa's eyes and spilled out onto her cheeks.

"But I don't like this idea of you talking to the media," he added. "You'd be making yourself a target."

"I already am one." She brushed away the tears and squared her shoulders. "Might as well make it count."

SIX

The next morning, Levi ushered Vanessa into the Torchlight Police Department headquarters. He held the door open and as she walked past, the light from an overhead fixture glinted on the bejeweled clip holding her hair in a ponytail. A smile crossed his lips. Now that he knew her story, he realized what a little bit of bling meant to her, that it was not a simple desire to be stylish as much as it was a determination not to let anyone stamp out her true spirit. With that in mind, he could appreciate the sparkle.

And that hint of rodeo woman flair was also a way she stayed connected to her late father.

The wallet they'd recovered would also be a connection to her father. Something real and tangible, and there was no telling what emotions would come to the surface when she saw it and actually touched it. So Levi wanted to ease into that rather than just handing it to her right away.

"Before we talk about your dad's case," he said, passing by her to lead the way to his desk, "I want to update you on our search for your attacker."

He gestured at a guest chair beside his desk. "Have a seat."

Vanessa sat and glanced around the office.

Pushed up against the front of Levi's desk and facing it was a second desk. And seated behind it was a uniformed young woman with short brown hair and bangs.

"Vanessa, this is Sergeant Melinda Ramirez. She's just been assigned to work with me on the investigation into the attack on you. Now that we're developing some leads on what happened to your father, she'll be working on that with me, as well."

Vanessa and the sergeant exchanged greetings.

"Melinda's spent some time looking at the available video from the hotel security cameras that were functioning properly the night you were attacked," Levi said. "She's also contacted the president of the Commerce Committee and acquired a list of the attendees on the night you were attacked at the Fargo Hotel. She's been calling and interviewing them."

"What have you learned?" Vanessa asked the sergeant.

Melinda had a pen in her hand and she tapped it on her desk a couple of times. "Well, we're still piecing things together. Right now I'm comparing timelines of who saw whom at what time. And when possible, I'm matching that up with the video. The information I have so far is sketchy. No one goes to an event like that expecting to give a description of what they were doing all evening. They may remember who they talked to but not be sure of the time. At Levi's suggestion, I'm focusing on Robert O'Connell."

Levi had been watching Vanessa closely, and at that point her gaze darted in his direction.

"Several people place Robert in the meeting room at the time of the attack on you over in the hallway," Melinda continued.

"But the security camera in the meeting room isn't placed very well," Levi interjected. "There's a blind spot near the passage into the hallway so we can't account for Robert's whereabouts one hundred percent of the time. It's possible people remember seeing him at the time the hotel employees found you unconscious. Not at the time you were attacked. Sometimes people honestly misremember things."

Vanessa looked at Levi for a few seconds with her lips pressed together. He got the impression she was running the information he'd just given her through her mind. Perhaps thinking about what she'd seen, coming up with her own timeline. With her being an attorney, it would be something she'd probably done or overseen often in working with her clients. Levi hoped it was a skill that would help in their attempts to uncover the person intent on harming her.

"Do you have a reason to suspect Robert O'Connell?" she finally asked. "Something you're not telling me?"

"No. But we can't overlook the fact that he was there, and knew in advance that you would be there, too."

They were not in a court of law. They were still investigating. Things were in flux. And there was an element of "gut instinct" in what he did. Not exactly something a lawyer, focused on fixed rules and facts, would typically appreciate.

"It's not like Robert would have a reason to rob my dad of his paycheck twenty years ago,"

Vanessa said. "And there's no reason for him to attack me now."

"True. But maybe the motive for your father's murder wasn't robbery."

Vanessa nodded thoughtfully, as though that idea had occurred to her before.

"We've recovered what is likely a piece of physical evidence from the attack on you at the hotel," he said.

Her eyes widened slightly in surprise. She was probably wondering why he hadn't told her sooner.

He had called her this morning, gone out to the ranch to get her and then driven her into town so that he would know she'd be safe. And in that time he had not mentioned the new evidence.

As a matter of practice, when Levi worked cases he limited the information he gave people over the phone, preferring to talk to them in person. Seeing their initial reaction and picking up what clues he could from that proved helpful. And he couldn't have seen that if he'd told her on the ride into town.

With Vanessa, he'd caught himself wanting to tell her more than he would normally tell a citizen he was working with. He wanted to treat her differently. Like a friend who needed his help. She'd worked hard to put tragedy behind her and he admired that. She hadn't given up hope over the long years while she'd waited for justice for her father. Hope was something people often let go of because it took courage to hold on to it. Vanessa was definitely a courageous woman.

But treating her like a personal friend while they worked on a case together was a bad idea in terms of professional ethics. And a worse idea in terms of his own personal well-being. It was more comfortable for him to keep his emotional distance. That way he didn't have to worry about making a stupid, selfish decision. Letting someone down. Not living up to the kind of standards he set for himself. So, no. He and Vanessa were not on the path to becoming friends. They were simply working together because it was a practical way to conduct two investigations. Besides, she lived in Las Vegas and she was returning soon.

So he'd withheld that little bit of information until they got to the station. Just to remind himself that theirs was a professional relationship. And to keep some reasonable emotional distance between them. If her surprise turned into annoyance with him, that might be a good thing.

"What did you find?" Vanessa asked.

"A signature Fargo Hotel table decoration. I'm sure you've seen them."

"Of course. Stagecoaches made out of bronze with the hotel name stamped on them. They use them to hold candles and floral centerpieces."

"And they're heavy enough to pack a punch if you swing one of them at someone."

Vanessa reached up to gingerly touch the back of her head. She winced slightly.

Her gesture and the reminder of the pain she'd suffered sent a surge of anger through Levi. But he bit back on the wave of emotion. He couldn't dwell on it. He needed to do his job and focus on finding the criminal who was attacking her.

"A member of the hotel grounds crew found the table decoration underneath some bushes just behind the hotel."

"Were you able to lift any fingerprints off it?"

"No," Levi answered. "It was wrapped in a couple of linen napkins. It was found very early this morning and forensics still has it. If you're willing to give blood and hair samples, we can confirm it was used to attack you."

The grim expression on her face told him

she was likely imagining what could have happened if the assailant had hit her with more force. Or on a different part of her head. The attack could have been fatal. "Of course." Her response was barely more than a whisper.

"The use of something already in the hotel as a weapon suggests whoever knocked you out didn't plan their attack ahead of time," Levi added. "He just saw a chance to attack you and took it. Like the attacker using the hammer when he chased you on the mesa."

"So, how does that fit into your investigation?" Vanessa asked, glancing back and forth between Levi and Sergeant Ramirez.

"We don't know yet," Levi answered. "It's a piece of the puzzle we'll set aside until we can start to guess where it fits."

An officer inside the squad room beckoned to Sergeant Ramirez. She stood up, excused herself and then walked over to talk to him.

"Now that you're updated on the investigation into the attacks on you," Levi said, "let's talk about your dad's case."

"Did your forensics team get anything from my dad's wallet that could help identify his killer?"

"No." But then, honestly, nobody had expected they would. "I still believe getting media attention for your dad's case might trigger people's memories and get us some new information. Especially about the fight Marv saw up on the mesa that night. The fact that your dad's wallet was found close by proves it wasn't a coincidence. Those men fighting knew something about your father's death." Levi glanced at his watch. "Sheila from the *Torchlight Beacon* should be here to talk to you in about twenty minutes. Are you still up for that?"

Vanessa nodded.

Already, the vulnerability and sorrow he'd seen expressed in her eyes and the set of her mouth was disappearing. She was likely shoring herself up and putting on the game face she used when she argued a case in court.

"I thought you might want to see the wallet before she gets here," Levi said. *Just in case you break down*, he thought, but didn't say. "I told Sheila she could photograph it and use the picture in the article. Maybe actually seeing this new evidence will prod a witness to come forward."

"Yes, I would like to see it now," Vanessa said.

Levi placed a quick call to the officer working the evidence room, then led Vanessa over there. “For the time being, I want to maintain close chain-of-custody protocols with the wallet,” Levi said. “Just to be cautious.”

Since the forensic work was completed, the wallet and its contents were stored in plastic bags so they could be visually examined but not physically touched.

The evidence officer brought the bags to the front counter where Vanessa could have a look.

Levi felt a sorrowful ache in his chest as he looked at the sad weathered bits of leather that had once belonged to her father. How would he feel in her situation? He couldn’t imagine. Both of his parents were alive. But he had lost close friends in combat and the memory of them would stay with him forever.

Maybe that was part of the reason why he found himself identifying with her and her situation so strongly. He knew what it was like to have someone you cared about die a violent death. How much you wanted to find answers and reasons. Maybe solving Josh Ford’s murder would feel like a kind of closure for Levi, too. A sense of justice and closure he never got to feel for his buddies lost in combat overseas.

He took a step back behind her, tried to give her what bit of privacy he could in an evidence room with a couple of other people milling around and working.

She lingered over the items and looked closely at them. She was tough, despite looking dainty and at times a little frilly. He'd learned at a young age that you couldn't tell what was on the inside of a person by looking at the outside. And yet, he was often surprised when he was reminded of that fact.

He heard her take a deep breath. Saw her shoulders rise and drop. Though he stood behind her, he could tell she was wiping tears from her face.

Finally, she turned around. Her eyes were red and watery, but the expression in them was one of steely determination. "I'm ready to talk to the reporter," she said. "Whatever it takes to bring the person who killed my father to justice. And to make sure no one else has to suffer the same loss I did."

After Vanessa's interview concluded and the reporter left, Levi suggested to Vanessa they go to the deli down the street to grab a quick bite to eat.

She didn't have much of an appetite, but she needed to eat something if she wanted to have the energy to keep working.

"If you've changed your mind and don't want to go through with this, I'll understand," Levi said to her as they walked back to the station after lunch.

"No," she told him. "I want to keep going."

The plan was to go through her father's case file, look at what was there and see if it triggered any memories or ideas for Vanessa. Maybe there'd be a familiar name or reference to an event she'd overheard grown-ups talking about when she was a kid. It could be that rumors she'd heard her mom or grandparents discussing in the past would be leads worth checking out now.

She'd already gotten promises from her mother and grandfather to let her know if they remembered something that could be helpful.

Levi got her seated at a conference table in a small meeting room, and then he went to get the boxes of cold-case notes from her father's original murder investigation. When he returned, he took a chair beside her so they could look at the items together.

Unease settled in her chest and her heartbeat sped up when he lifted the lid off the first box. She didn't know what she was afraid of. Maybe the possibility there was some grim bit of information in that box that would cause her heart to break all over again.

At least she had Levi beside her. His calm, steady demeanor in every situation had already soothed her more than once. "For now, let's take a fairly quick check of everything in here and see what we have," Levi said. "I'll comb through everything again much more slowly, and more than once, after you've gone home to Las Vegas."

Together, they looked over the notes and narratives, government forms and press clippings that told the story of what had happened as far as anyone knew. Vanessa and Levi each made comments or voiced questions as they thought of them. Levi took notes on an electronic tablet.

"There are several interviews here with employees on the O'Connell ranch," Levi said, tapping the binder in front of him. "A couple of them mention that Robert O'Connell's son, Trent, was a hothead and that he and your dad didn't get along." He shuffled through some of the other papers on the table. "I don't see notes from an interview with Trent in here."

Vanessa sat back in her chair, thinking for a moment. "I believe he left town for college around that time."

"Huh," Levi said.

"What are you thinking?" Vanessa asked.

"Just that I want to talk to him." He typed a few notes into his tablet. "I also want to interview your stepfather."

"I don't even know where he lives."

"I found an address for him in Fresno, California," Levi said. "I'll start with a telephone interview and see where that leads."

"All right."

Levi set his tablet aside. "I know this is a lot to process, emotionally. Do you want to stop?"

"No. There isn't much more to look at in the second box. I just need a short break." She stood and stretched her back. "I saw that Eddie Scott was cleared as a suspect because he was at work at the time of my dad's murder. But we still haven't come across anything telling us specifically why Kenny Goren was dropped as a viable suspect."

They'd already seen notes about him, explaining why he'd been considered as a possibility. He'd been picked up for various assaults and petty thefts from the time he was a juvenile. He was twenty-five at the time of the murder. A witness claimed to have seen him up on the mesa the night of the murder and later flashing cash around at a bar in town.

"I ran a background check on Goren to see what he's been up to in the years since your father was murdered," Levi said. "He has been in and out of prison for burglary, fencing stolen goods and strong-arm robbery over the course of about twelve years. After the last stint, he completed his time on parole without incident and there's been nothing since then. At least nothing he was *caught* doing."

"Strong-arm robbery," Vanessa echoed. "Maybe my dad was one of his first victims."

"Maybe." Then he stood. "I'm going to grab a cup of coffee," Levi said. "Would you like one?"

"Sounds perfect." Vanessa's head was starting to pound. As an attorney, she was used to keeping a lot of facts straight in her mind. But when the grim facts involved your own family, the possibilities of what might have happened could race around in your head until they all joined together into one big blur.

After a couple of sips of coffee a few minutes later, she felt a bit revived.

The last binder did indeed have some notes about Kenny Goren. "The witness who claimed to see Goren on the mesa and in town was a known criminal and enemy of Goren," Levi said, looking down at the notes. "No one else corroborated his story. Goren claimed he was eating dinner, alone, at a local pizza joint the night of the murder and an acquaintance testified she'd seen him there. With no physical evidence and an unreliable witness statement, the police were compelled to release him and not press charges."

"I'd like to talk to the witness who claimed she saw Goren at the pizza place," Vanessa said. "Maybe she lied about that. Maybe she was his girlfriend."

Levi leaned back in his chair, finished the dregs of his coffee and set the cup on the table. "I'd like to talk to Kenny Goren. After I take you back to the ranch, I'm going to pay him a visit."

"I'm going with you." Vanessa got to her feet and pushed her shoulders back, determined to look like the capable woman that she was. She didn't want Levi to get used to seeing her as a pitiful woman whose father had been murdered. She'd worked too hard to *not* be pitiful. Plus, she was still certain her involvement in the investigation would get them some new information and help break her father's case wide open. She couldn't imagine that a man who had been in and out of jail for years would be forthcoming with a policeman.

Levi stayed seated, calmly looking up at her and slowly shaking his head. "Kenny Goren has a history of violence. He might have murdered your father and he could have already attacked you. Twice."

Vanessa cleared her throat. "If you're trying to scare me, it's working. But I know something about career criminals. They hate cops and won't talk to them. They aren't usually crazy about lawyers, either. But there's a slight chance he'll talk to me, so I'm willing to try it." She crossed her arms over her chest. "And maybe if I see him and talk to him, I'll be able to tell if he's the man who chased me on the mesa."

Levi looked at her closely for a moment and then got to his feet. "I'll go see what the chief thinks."

Forty minutes later Levi turned the police SUV into the driveway of a business that looked like a dumping ground with a cinder block building and a house trailer at one end. Vanessa rode beside him in the passenger seat. Sergeant Ramirez and another officer followed behind them in a patrol car.

"'Buy, Sell or Trade Anything,'" Vanessa read aloud from the hand-painted sign. It was attached to the building above a roll-up door on what appeared to be a former auto-repair shop. "What an original name for a business," she added dryly.

"I can only imagine how many stolen goods have passed through here," Levi muttered.

Ramirez got out of her patrol car and walked toward Levi's SUV. The officer with Ramirez also got out, but remained standing beside the car.

"Sergeant Ramirez and I are going to try to talk to Goren first," Levi said. "Officer Farwell is staying out here to keep an eye on you, just to be safe. If Goren won't talk to us, I'll come get you."

"Got it." Vanessa watched Levi and Ramirez walk into the building. From where she sat she couldn't see inside.

Fifteen minutes passed but it felt like an hour. Finally, Levi came outside and walked up to Vanessa's side of the SUV. She rolled down the window. "Goren claims he doesn't have anything to say to us," Levi told her. "Do you still want to try and get him to talk? It's fine if you don't. I have no doubt if we look around, we'll find something here that's been reported stolen and we can use that as leverage to get him to cooperate. It just might take a little while."

"I'll talk to him." Vanessa got out of the SUV.

The lighting inside the shop was dim and it took a few seconds for Vanessa's eyes to adjust. There weren't any customers around. Just a man in his midforties with obviously dyed black hair and a scraggly matching mustache. He sat in an old office chair and watched her curiously. Kenny Goren. She recognized him from his police booking photos.

Vanessa wanted to appear tough in front of him, but despite her best intentions, she took a step back when she felt the uncomfortable weight of his gaze settle on her.

Fortunately, Levi made for a very comforting backstop.

"I know who you are," Goren said.

The tiny hairs on the back of Vanessa's neck stood on end. Still, she would be strong despite her fear and focus on the task at hand. *Dear Lord, please help me.*

She hadn't expected Goren's voice to sound familiar. But she'd hoped for something in the cadence or tone that she could latch onto. But there was nothing.

"If you know who I am, you can probably guess why I'm here," Vanessa said. "May I ask you some questions?"

A twisted grin crossed Goren's lips and then

he reached up to scratch at his mustache. His gaze darted to Levi, who was standing behind Vanessa, and then to Ramirez.

The grin disappeared from Goren's face and his expression went blank. Vanessa knew he was about to dismiss her without answering her questions.

"I didn't kill your old man," he finally said. "And Josh Ford was no saint. Just so you know."

Vanessa braced herself for whatever else he might say, knowing any or all of it could be a lie.

"Do you know who did kill him?" she managed to ask in a steady voice.

"I know your dad was a pretty boy with good manners and the ladies liked that. Could be an angry husband or boyfriend came after him."

Vanessa was itching to redirect him back to answering the question of what he actually *knew*, but she didn't do it. Sometimes it was better to let someone keep talking.

"Your old man had a smart mouth, too," Goren added. "That made a few people mad."

Despite the situation, Vanessa found herself biting back a grin. So *that* was where her unfortunate tendency to speak before she thought had come from. She'd inherited it from her dad.

"How did you know my dad?" she asked. "Did you work up at the O'Connell ranch?"

"On and off. As a day laborer. I don't know anything about horses. Those cowboys all thought they were better than anybody else. Especially the boss's kid. Trent. It's a shame somebody didn't knock off *him*."

Goren quickly shifted his gaze to Levi. "Not that I'm advocating violence."

"Did you happen to get into a fight on the mesa the night my dad was murdered?" Vanessa asked.

Goren scrunched his eyebrows closer together. "No. Why?"

His confusion seemed genuine, so Vanessa figured it was a dead end and decided to skip an explanation. He could read all about the reported fight on the mesa online after her interview was posted tomorrow morning.

"Did you see or hear anything that might help me find out who killed my dad?"

Goren leaned back in his squeaky office chair and tilted his head to the side. "There's all kinds of people that drift through town looking for work and end up with a job on a ranch. Here today, gone tomorrow. It was probably a drifter desperate for money who killed your old man. And you ain't ever gonna find him."

Aware that she might need to talk to him again, Vanessa didn't tell him what she thought of his opinion. Instead, she turned and spoke quietly over her shoulder to Levi, "Let's go."

She turned to Goren. "Thank you." And then started for the door.

Behind her, she heard Levi ask Goren, "Have you ever been inside the Fargo Hotel?"

Vanessa turned back to watch the exchange. Goren's face was a study in anger and contempt as he glared at Levi, his mouth closed tight and his lips a thin pale line. He refused to say a word.

Vanessa took a deep breath and blew it out once they were outside.

"You all right?" Levi asked as they climbed back into his SUV and watched Ramirez get back into her patrol car.

No. She was not all right. She was sad, and angry, and disappointed and afraid. She was also creeped out by Goren. But she didn't want to tell Levi that. Not after he'd gone out of his way to include her in the police investigation. She didn't want to lie to him, either. So she forced a smile.

He did not smile back. The thoughtful expression in his dark brown eyes told her he knew exactly how she really felt.

SEVEN

"You ready to ride?" Sam Ford sat tall in the saddle on the back of one of the recently arrived horses, a gentle palomino named Stardust, and grinned at Pablo.

Pablo, astride another of the new arrivals, a fidgety buckskin named Bluebonnet, returned the grin. "Yes, I am."

Vanessa watched them, delight bubbling up within her. It was already helping to chase away the gloom that had settled in last night after meeting Kenny Goren.

Seeing Grandpa happy made Vanessa happy.

"Wish I was going with you," she said. When Grandpa's smile faltered, she immediately gave herself a swift mental kick. He didn't need the reminder that she was in danger. That some unidentified psychopath was intent on doing her harm. She might not be thrilled with having to stay close to the house on such a beautiful day, but she did want to stay alive. And she wanted her grandpa to have a good time.

"I'll just wait until after you two have done all the work getting the trails cleared and then I'll go riding," she added in a teasing tone.

The ranch property meandered around just over two hundred acres. Not big, for this part of the country, but big enough for their purposes. The previous owners had established a riding trail that looped around the property, through forest, across some good-sized ponds and across the Torchlight River. Nobody had ridden the complete trail since winter. Grandpa and Pablo were going to ride it and take note of fallen trees or large branches that they'd need to clear before their first guests arrived in three weeks.

"I think Bluebonnet here is ready for us to stop yapping and start riding." Pablo gave his horse a couple of reassuring pats on the neck as she shuffled around a little. The plan was to get the new horses out on the trail, a couple at a time, and let them get used to the lay of the land.

Maybelle had been standing at the edge of the corral, watching what was going on. She nickered softly.

"We'll get you out walking the trail once

we're sure it's safe," Sam hollered over to the old horse.

She'd been getting special treatment from him, in the form of the apples that she loved, every day. He was worried she might be feeling left out with the arrival of the new horses.

The sounds of hammers and power tools carried across the property where the cabins were nearly finished and the Dinner Bell Dining Hall, which would house dining facilities and a common room where guests could mingle and enjoy fun activities, was well underway. The construction manager had done an excellent job so far and the projects were right on schedule.

"So, go riding already," Vanessa said to her grandpa and Pablo as she made a shooing motion.

She didn't have to ask them twice. Both men gave their horses a light kick and started toward the trail, whooping and hollering like kids as their animals picked up steam.

"What are those crazy old men doing with all that yelling?" Rosa strode out of the house, smiling and shaking her head. "It's like they're living a second childhood." She watched them ride off until they disappeared behind the trees. Her black-framed reading glasses rode low on her nose and she carried several sheets of paper in her hand.

"They're just enjoying life."

Rosa lifted her chin and peered at Vanessa through her glasses. "You'll be able to enjoy life again. Your *friend* Levi will catch whoever is after you."

Rosa grinned but Vanessa refused to take the bait. She and Levi were working together. That was it.

Slowly Rosa's grin faded and she blew out a sigh. "Don't lose faith, honey."

"I'm not." Levi had called earlier. Her interview and the pictures of her father's recovered wallet had been published in the paper this morning and had already generated a few phone calls and emails to the police department. Levi and Sergeant Ramirez would be following up on them, as well as revisiting the boxes of case notes and combing through all the information in them a little more slowly and carefully. "I know it's going to take time to find the person who's been after me and to find my dad's killer," Vanessa added.

The thought struck her that she needed to do more praying, too. For the hardworking people in the police department. And for her friends and family.

All of the things dragging down her spirit could be lifted up in prayer. That didn't mean she would necessarily get the answers she wanted. But it would remind her that she wasn't in control of everything. That little bit of humbling herself always did wonders in lifting the weight of heavy burdens from her shoulders.

Vanessa indicated the papers in Rosa's hand. "What have you got there?"

"A booking for a family reunion. They want to reserve all the cabins, the campsites, the whole place."

Bookings had slowly been trickling in and that was a relief. The property plus the expenditures it took to turn it into a guest ranch cost some serious money. Which meant Vanessa needed to get back to work in Vegas as soon as possible so she could keep kicking in her share of the expenses until the business started earning.

"One family wants to book the whole place?" Vanessa asked. "Must be a good-sized family."

"More like a good-hearted family. The lady who booked it said they're bringing some friends along, too. Specifically friends who don't have much in the way of blood-kin."

Vanessa felt herself smile. There were good people in the world. When traumatic things happened at the hands of someone intent on doing evil, it was easy to forget that.

"I'm gonna grab the rest of my stuff out of my car." Vanessa gestured toward her sedan, sporting four brand-new tires, parked several yards from the front door of the ranch house. It had been returned to her the day after the attack on the mesa, but she hadn't taken the time until now to unpack it. "Might as well do something useful and get my bedroom spruced up since I'll be staying in the house all day."

She broadened her smile as she turned toward Rosa to make it clear she wasn't complaining about having to stay inside so she wouldn't be an easy target for another attack. Vanessa's work at the women's shelter in Vegas reminded her on a regular basis that some women didn't even have a safe place to hunker down.

"Do you need help?"

Vanessa shook her head. "It's just two boxes and they aren't very heavy."

She'd brought a few small things that she'd kept with her in Las Vegas. Items with sentimental value. A framed picture of her with both her parents. A torn and threadbare stuffed tiger with a missing ear her grandparents had given her for Christmas when she was five.

The ugly table lamp from her dorm room that reminded her of how hard she'd worked to get through college and then law school.

She walked to the car and popped open the trunk.

When Grandpa insisted she lay claim to a small upstairs bedroom at the ranch house, she realized the ranch was the best place for all her treasures. It was where they belonged. Leaving them here would remind her to come back. If the person targeting her thought he would chase her away from Torchlight and her family forever, he was wrong.

She grabbed the two boxes, then using her left arm to hold most of their weight, she used her right elbow to close the trunk lid. She turned and started walking back toward the house. The things she wanted in her room that weren't sentimental, like furniture, paint and window treatments, had been ordered online and shipped ahead, arriving a few days before she did. Grandpa and Pablo had put the bed together and lugged the dresser and chest of drawers up the stairs. Rosa had hung the curtains. For now, she'd put these boxes in the closet and get started painting.

Walking across thick grass, enjoying the warm sunshine and vibrant blue Nevada sky,

Vanessa felt something smack her left shoulder. The burning impact twisted her upper body, wrenching the boxes from her hands and spilling the contents. She was forced to take a couple of stumbling steps backward.

Stunned and confused, her breath caught in her throat.

And then mixed in with the sounds of hammering and power tools as the workers put together the guest cabins, she heard the report of a rifle shot.

No.

The construction sounds slowed to a stop.

And then a second projectile whizzed by, plowing up a chunk of grass behind her. The crack of the rifle shot reached her ears loud and clear. The shooter was close. She couldn't draw in enough breath to scream. Couldn't think which way to move.

She heard the construction manager yelling at everyone to get down and saw the workers crouch beside their vehicles or the guest cabins where they were working.

The shots sounded like they were coming from the nearby forested hill to the south of the ranch.

She was standing closer to a supply shed than she was to the house.

Desperate to find cover before she was hit again, she doubled over, ran to the shed and dived down beside it since the door seemed to be directly in the line of fire. She yelped as she hit the hard ground and jolted her injured shoulder.

Sucking in air through clenched teeth as the pain in her shoulder echoed throughout her body, she glanced toward the house. Rosa stood at the window, looking toward Vanessa. She had the curtain pushed aside with her elbow while she held a phone up to her ear in one hand and held a long gun in the other.

She must be talking to 9-1-1.

Vanessa had left her own phone in the house. Not that she thought her hands would be steady enough to dial a phone right now. Her shoulder burned and the fabric of her blouse, damp with blood, stuck to her skin.

At the window, Rosa made a gesture as if she wanted to come out and help Vanessa.

Vanessa held up a staying hand. She was in a safe spot. All the workers were hidden from view. No more shots had been fired. The police had to be on their way. It would be best for everyone to continue to stay in place.

Yet another rifle shot blew that plan all to pieces. It came from a slightly different direction so that Vanessa was no longer protected by the shed. A slight adjustment by the shooter could place the next bullet right between her eyes.

This wasn't someone just trying to scare her anymore. This was someone trying to kill her.

But which way should she go? Which way was safety and which way might put her directly in the crosshairs of the shooter?

Could there be a *second* shooter?

If so, she was in danger no matter which direction she went. She longed for the sturdy protection of the ranch house, not to mention the comforting companionship of being in there alongside Rosa. But getting inside the shed she was hiding behind seemed the wiser choice. Pushing herself to her feet, she ran to the door, fumbled with the latch, yanked it open and then darted inside and shut the door behind her.

Could the bullets from the rifle shots penetrate the thin metal sides of the shed? She had no idea, so she literally hit the dirt, ignoring the dull pain that came with smacking her knees on the rocks in the hard-packed soil. At least there were shelves lining the walls, holding old tools, coffee cans full of nails and bolts, and offering some kind of barricade in front of the small windows on each side.

Her shoulder throbbed. Or maybe it was her heart pounding so hard in fear that its jack-hammer rhythm pulsed throughout her whole body. She gasped for breath while straining to hear any noise that would tell her what was happening. *Dear Lord, please protect us all.*

She listened for the sound of sirens, but the odds of a cop car already being in the vicinity were remote. She hadn't even considered asking for police protection while she was here on the ranch. There were so many people around, all potential witnesses. As long as she stayed close to the house, she'd thought she was safe.

For a brief few seconds, her thoughts went back to the attack at the Fargo Hotel. Who would be desperate enough to take such huge public risks in attacking her? And why?

It took her a few seconds to realize she hadn't heard any more rifle shots. Was that a good or a bad thing? Could it mean the shooter was creeping closer to the flimsy building where she was hiding?

As the thought crossed her mind, she heard a sound by the door of the shed. She felt the blood drain from her face. Unable to put much pressure on her injured shoulder, she did her best to scoot away from the door and into a corner. She frantically looked around in the dim light for something she could use to defend herself. She grabbed the edge of a can filled with bolts and screws and got ready to fling it.

The door shoved open. A figure crouched down low in the doorframe. “Vanessa?”

Relief washed over her and she loosened her grip on the can. “Grandpa.”

He came the rest of the way in, shut the door behind him and hurried over to her, dropping to his knees in the dirt beside her. “Thank the Lord,” he whispered as he wrapped an arm around her shoulder.

She yelped and he leaned back, trying to look at her injured shoulder in the shadowy corner where they sat.

“I’m pretty sure it’s already stopped bleeding,” she said.

He tore off the tail of his shirt, balled up the fabric and pressed it against her wound. “Just in case,” he muttered.

“How did you know I was here?”

“Pablo had his phone. Rosa called him on the house phone while she was staying with the 9-1-1 operator on her cell. We left the horses back a ways and came up here on foot.”

The faint sound of a dog barking and people talking caught their attention and both of them stood to cautiously peer out the window. An officer with a K-9 moved around the low hill in the distance where the shots had first seemed to originate. Several other officers searched with them.

In the area close to the cabins and guest facilities, construction workers came out from where they'd taken cover and started calling out to one another.

Farther out, Vanessa saw Levi's police SUV racing along the driveway leading to the house. An ambulance followed behind him at a more cautious speed since the location wasn't secure yet. Levi bypassed the ranch house and pulled up directly in front of the shed. His vehicle came to a sudden sliding stop. He got out and ran to the door.

Levi's hands trembled slightly as he accepted a cup of coffee from Rosa. Adrenaline still raced through his bloodstream. The icy fear that had gut-punched him when he'd first heard Vanessa had been shot was keeping its grip on his chest. He was determined to remain calm, to be of comfort to Vanessa, and so he was sitting on a floral sofa in the family room of the ranch house and sipping coffee when he wanted to be outside in the surrounding wilderness, tracking the would-be killer.

He glanced at Vanessa, seated beside him, her shoulder wrapped in bandages, courtesy of the paramedic. She wore one of her grandfather's flannel shirts, which was loose on her and didn't put pressure on the wound. He could tell by the expression on her face that she'd seen his hands shaking.

"I'm all right," she whispered. She moved her hand, which she'd had resting on the couch, so that the tips of her fingers brushed his knuckles ever so slightly.

Her touch managed to both strengthen and weaken him at the same time.

Sam Ford was pacing back and forth across the living room floor, focused on something only he could see. Pablo likewise drifted back and forth between the room's two largest windows, watching the officers still working in the distance. Rosa was obviously trying to create a calm atmosphere by bringing out cups of coffee and plates of cookies from the kitchen. But she also had her rifle propped in the corner of the room.

Levi's phone chimed and he glanced at a text from Ramirez on the screen.

Still haven't found signs or tracks of a second shooter.

He read it aloud to Vanessa.

"I thought there might be two," she said. "But maybe not." She pursed her lips and thought for a minute. "I don't know. Right now, it's all kind of a blur."

"You might remember more later on," Rosa said, finally sitting down in the easy chair.

Sam stopped his pacing and crossed his arms over his chest, ignoring the coffee Rosa had set on an end table near him.

"The K-9 found the sniper's nest on the hill to the south where the original shots came from," Levi said, glancing in Sam's direction. "It looks like the shooter waited there for a while to get a good shot. The vegetation is tramped down and spent casings were left behind. So it doesn't look like the work of a professional. Otherwise, there'd be no trace of him left."

Beside Levi, Vanessa's breath hitched. Part of him wanted to edit what he'd said to spare her feelings. But she'd told him she wanted to know everything he could tell her, and he respected that. She was mentally and emotionally strong. He didn't doubt that about her despite everything that had happened. He'd spent enough time around her to know that was true.

"We can talk about that some more later,"

Sam said, looking at his granddaughter. "Right now, I want to get you to the hospital for some stitches."

Vanessa was willing to go to the hospital for further treatment, but she was not willing to go there in an ambulance.

"I'd like to take her. It would be safer," Levi said, getting to his feet. "She'll be riding in a police vehicle. I'll have another patrol car go with us."

Vanessa stood up, wobbling a little. Levi reached out to steady her.

"I don't care who takes me," she said irritably. "I shouldn't have to keep going through this. Let's just get it done."

Levi's gaze lingered on her face. She had a right to be frustrated. Her blue eyes looked dark and sunken. Her skin was chalky. "We'll both take you," he said, glancing at Sam. "In my SUV."

Levi stayed close by her side, holding on to her arm as they walked out to his vehicle. Vanessa sat in the passenger side and her grandfather sat in the back. After taking a minute to contact dispatch and let them know where he was going and what he was doing, they headed out to the highway and then to Torchlight. He made sure one of the patrol cars at the ranch followed them.

It was a quiet ride into town. Levi intentionally didn't ask Vanessa any more questions about the shooting and instead let her take the lead on what she wanted to say. She didn't seem to want to say much. He didn't blame her.

He stayed as close to her as possible at the hospital while still allowing her some privacy. Possible scenarios of what exactly had happened at the ranch today passed through his mind. Vanessa could be misremembering the seeming change in the direction that the shots were fired from. Or the person who'd attacked her on the mesa and in the Fargo Hotel might have taken on a partner. That would be a huge game changer.

Levi was pretty well convinced the attacker on the mesa and at the Fargo Hotel were the same person. It was possible the interview she'd given the *Torchlight Beacon* had scared someone completely new out of the woodwork. The online version of the story had been available since late last night. Maybe someone was afraid a person who'd witnessed the fight on the mesa the night of Josh Ford's murder would step forward. Maybe if someone could identify the two men fighting on the mesa, it would provide a lead that would solve the case.

Perhaps their conversation with Kenny Goren last night had pushed the man who had been a prime suspect all those years ago over the edge. Levi tapped the screen on his phone to call Chief Haskell. Somebody needed to go by and pay Kenny a visit tonight, just to see if there was anything suspicious going on with him.

While he waited for the chief to pick up his call, Levi thought about the danger Vanessa faced. It had never occurred to him that she would be unsafe at the ranch. He had to do something to make sure she was protected.

Not long after his conversation with the chief ended, Vanessa walked out of the ER with a couple of prescriptions and reassurances that while her gunshot wound was painful, none of the underlying muscles or bones had been damaged and her biggest concern was avoiding infection.

When they were all back in his police SUV, Levi offered to take them to get something to eat while they were still in town, but neither Vanessa nor her grandfather was hungry. He started up the engine and cleared his throat. "Mr. Ford," he said, looking in his rearview mirror until he could see Sam looking back at him. "Would it be all right with you if I parked a travel trailer beside your house at the ranch and stayed there?" Vanessa had been looking at her prescription bottles. She set them down in her lap and turned her gaze toward him.

"I think it would be best if Vanessa had some additional protection for a while," Levi added. "Given everything that's happened." Levi turned to Vanessa. "Is that all right with you?"

She nodded. "I'd appreciate it."

Levi turned his gaze back to the mirror so he could see Sam, waiting for his approval.

"You aren't bringing a trailer out to the ranch to live in," Sam said. "You can just move into the house."

EIGHT

Vanessa stood looking out the window of the ranch house, watching the headlights drawing closer. Levi had called ahead while he was still on the highway to let her know he'd be approaching in a couple of minutes.

Everyone in the house had been jumpy in the two days since the shooting. Even now, Vanessa stood at the window with her body mostly hidden by the thick curtain, peering out into the darkness and anxiously searching for the markings that would confirm she was looking at a police vehicle.

Finally, she could see the Torchlight Police Department insignia on the passenger-side door. She sighed and let the curtain fall back into place as she turned away from the window. The odds that it was someone other than Levi were ridiculously low. Her rational brain knew that. But since she'd been shot, it felt like the logical, analytical Vanessa had been replaced by a version of herself that jumped at every loud noise and constantly thought she saw something suspicious from the corner of her eye.

From the den, she heard the laugh track from the TV show Rosa was watching. When she'd gone in to tell Rosa about Levi's call, Pablo had been sound asleep in the easy chair beside her with both cats curled up on his lap.

Grandpa had gone upstairs to bed after Rosa and Pablo promised to stay up and keep Vanessa company until Levi arrived. They'd been treating her with kid gloves yesterday and today while she'd read through the files and interview transcripts Levi had sent to her while he was working at the police station. He'd insisted she stay home and rest, but she'd had enough of that. Having old friends call to check on her was nice, but she really wanted to dive back into the investigation alongside Levi.

A very disturbed person was trying to harm her. *Kill* her. Hiding here at the ranch for the rest of her life or running back to Las Vegas wouldn't guarantee she would be out of danger. Or that the people she loved would be safe.

She'd spent some of the afternoon praying and reading Psalms. Both activities had strengthened her. And reminded her of the power of faith.

But inevitably, fear wriggled its way back into her mind. The battle to keep from giving in to dismay and anxiety was far from over. But she would trust God to continue on.

A key turned in the lock on the front door. For the time being, they were keeping all doors that led outside locked.

Levi pushed the door open and stepped in, his gaze sweeping the front room until it settled on her. She saw his shoulders drop a little, as though he was relieved to see her.

She felt the same way about seeing him. Relieved. But also safe. Comforted. Protected.

Because he's a cop, she told herself. Though that didn't really have anything to do with the delighted quivering sensation in the pit of her stomach. Now it felt like her nerves were on edge in a different way. Almost as if…

No. This feeling was just that. Only a feeling. It was not the basis of a relationship. He was working hard to keep her safe and they were spending a lot of time together. Of course that would generate feelings. Like reassurance when she saw him. But those feelings would gradually fade once the crisis had passed. Once he returned to his normal life and responsibilities just as she would return to her normal life.

Their lives would stay separate because they lived in different ends of the state. And Vanessa had already had her fill of trying to make a romantic relationship work. Who was she kidding? She hadn't really had much experience with an actual romantic relationship. The truth was she'd dated a few times but things had never clicked. Maybe she would try again someday. Although her current experiences were making it look more and more like she'd always be different from most people and find relationships difficult because of what she'd been through.

"Hi," Levi called out before turning to lock the door.

"Hello," Vanessa responded.

He put a take-out bag from a fast-food place in town on the table. "As I was driving up I was thinking you should get a couple of dogs out here," he said. "To alert you when anybody's coming up to the house."

"We plan to. But we thought it would be wise to wait until the new buildings are complete and the new horses are settled in and everybody is used to the routine of having guests and running the business." She ambled over to peer into the food bags. Burgers and fries. Nothing very exciting. "Rosa made chiles rellenos. Wouldn't you rather have some of that?"

"I already invited myself into your home and helped myself to several meals here. I appreciate it, but I really don't expect you to feed me."

"Don't be ridiculous." She rolled the food bag tightly closed and slid it across to the far end of the table.

Tornado darted into the room and then came to a sudden stop on a throw rug, crouching down and flicking his tail. A few seconds later, Rosa followed the gray cat into the room.

"We're getting Levi some dinner," Vanessa said after Rosa and Levi exchanged greetings.

"Good. Pablo's awake and I'm here for ice cream." Rosa pointed to Tornado. "And that little hooligan is in trouble for scratching a chair."

All three of them went into the kitchen. Tornado followed, not looking the slightest bit contrite.

Rosa grabbed a couple of bowls out of the cabinet, then a scoop and spoons from a drawer and finally the salted-caramel ice cream from the freezer. As she scooped the ice cream, Tornado wove back and forth between her ankles. Possibly hoping for a handout.

Rosa headed back to the den with her bowls

of ice cream. Vanessa dished up some chiles rellenos and Mexican rice on a plate for Levi, set it in the microwave and hit the button for it to start. Then she got herself some ice cream.

"How are you holding up?" Levi asked, leaning against the kitchen counter while Vanessa poured chocolate syrup all over her ice cream.

"I'm doing all right." She took a bite of ice cream and found herself surprisingly disappointed. Usually she really enjoyed this combination. But over the last few days, most food had lost its appeal.

She dropped her spoon into the bowl and it made a loud clanking sound. Why should she hide her true feelings from Levi? If hearing about them was too much for him, so what? It's not like she was planning a future with him.

"Actually, I'm not doing so well. I'm worried everything is falling apart. The construction workers aren't coming back anytime soon. Understandably. Not until we're certain they'll be safe." She shook her head. "It doesn't matter, anyway. Several people who'd made reservations for next month when we're scheduled to open called to cancel. Rosa called the rest to let them know what happened. She thought it was the right thing to do. Of course, nobody wants to stay here until the bad guy is caught. And I don't blame them."

"We'll catch whoever is doing this to you," Levi said. The microwave timer buzzed. Levi walked over to remove his food and brought it to the table.

Vanessa pulled out the chair across from him and sat down. "The attacks on me must be related to my father's murder. Nothing else makes sense." She stirred her ice cream. "By the way, thank you for forwarding the emails."

"Of course." He bowed his head for a few seconds before picking up his fork and digging into the food.

Levi had forwarded to Vanessa a few of the emails her interview had generated. Roughly half were from people offering condolences. People who knew her dad or were touched by his tragic murder back when it was originally in the news.

The rest were from people who had theories or had heard rumors that made them think they might be able to identify the two men who were fighting on the mesa that night. Levi had wanted to know if Vanessa recognized any of the names. She hadn't.

And thinking about that made her feel like the energy was draining out of her body. This battle to find out who was attacking her could take a long time to be solved. Or it might not ever be solved. She could be stalked and threatened for the rest of her life. And her dad's murderer might not ever be brought to justice.

She stared glumly at her bowl of melting ice cream. There were moments when it felt like the flavor had been sucked out of every aspect of her life. Her eyes began to burn and she could feel tears welling up.

"Tell me what you're thinking right now," Levi said calmly before scooping up a forkful of spicy rice.

She wasn't sure she could put it into words. Instead, she looked down at her injured shoulder. She was feeling sorry for herself, though she didn't really want to. Finally, she just shook her head.

"You've been shot." Levi laid down his fork and looked her square in the eye. "That shouldn't happen to any human being, but it does."

"It's happened to you?" Vanessa asked softly.

He nodded. "In combat. And it gets you thinking about man's inhumanity to man and all kinds of dark stuff. Your feelings are bound to be all over the place. Plus, there's the effect of all the medicines in your body. Give it time. You'll feel better."

She looked away. Her brain knew he was probably right. He had the life experience to know what he was talking about. But at the moment she didn't want to be soothed. She wanted to fight back. To push back against all the evil intentions in the world.

"It's only been a few days since our interview was published," he added. "There's still a good chance that somebody will come forth with some solid, helpful information about the fight on the mesa. Or anything at all connected to your dad's murder."

"I'm surprised you believe people will be that helpful." She sounded like a moody adolescent and she felt like one. Knowing the reasons why, and that the feelings would pass, didn't change that. "You're a cop. Shouldn't you be more cynical?"

From the way he looked at her she knew she'd struck a nerve. "I'm sorry, I shouldn't have said that." She couldn't let herself indulge in this anxious, impatient feeling any longer. It wasn't fair to Levi. Or anyone else who was around her and was trying to help.

"You know, I did try giving in to cynicism for a while after I came home from the army."

He paused, and in the quiet Vanessa could hear the refrigerator humming. She wasn't sure she wanted to hear anything personal from him. About his life experiences. Because if it brought them closer, that would also make it that much harder when they went their separate ways.

"For a while, I carried a deep-seated conviction that people all over the world were jerks," he continued. "Of course, I sought out situations to prove it was true. And in the process I became a pretty big jerk myself."

She arched an eyebrow. "And here I thought this was going to be an uplifting story."

A soft laugh escaped him, turning his serious expression into something more approachable. "My point is, you think you're going to protect yourself from disappointment if you're cynical, but you don't."

"All right."

He took a deep breath and blew it out. "I told you I was in California. What I didn't tell you was that when I got back stateside, I moved to California with some friends. I partied too hard and too often. One night, a drinking buddy was racing his motorcycle up Pacific Coast Highway and misjudged a curve in the road. He didn't survive."

Vanessa thought about what he'd told her when they were up on the mesa after they'd talked to Marv. When he'd tried to tell her he wasn't a hero because he'd gone through a season in his life when he'd let people down. This must have been in that same time frame.

He paused and bit down on his bottom lip for a minute. "There was a funeral. Walking up the steps and into the church, I had a pretty callous attitude. I remember thinking, 'you win some, and you lose some.' But once I was inside, I started to pray for the first time in a long time. It took a while, but eventually I threw aside that cynicism, and it was like a slab of concrete had been lifted off of me. I found I still had hope in my heart. That included hope for the best in other people. I decided I wanted to keep it."

Vanessa shifted in her seat. "This isn't the first time I've been tempted to harden my heart. But you're right. It wouldn't protect me. Not really. And it wouldn't make my life any better."

He picked up his fork to resume eating.

She didn't want to stare at him while he ate. But she didn't want to get up and walk away, either. So she glanced around the kitchen, taking in the sight of the cookie jar shaped like a rooster and the hand towel with the sunflowers hanging from the handle on the refrigerator door. The coffeepot was nearly as old as she was, but for some reason made the best coffee in the world. They were all things her grandparents had brought from their old house. Things that made this ranch feel like home.

"How's your shoulder?" Levi asked.

"It itches where they stitched me up."

"That's a good sign. It means it's healing." He pointed at her bowl with his fork. "Aren't you going to eat the rest of your ice cream?"

Most of it was melted, so when she stirred it the result was something like a chocolate milkshake. But this time when she took a taste, it wasn't so bad.

"It's oddly relaxing to be able to talk to someone about my father's murder, someone who isn't a family member, and not have them freak out," she said. Even the people she thought of as close friends avoided mentioning her dad. Some avoided talking about their own dads when they were around her. Probably trying to be considerate.

"I'm fortunate to have people I can talk to about my combat experience," Levi said. "It helps."

"You can talk to me," she said, feeling shy about making the offer.

He settled his gaze on her, let it linger, and she felt a soft, fluttery feeling in the center of her chest.

"I guess I've already talked your ear off about my dad," she added, because sitting in silence with him, which had never been a problem before, was now making her nervous.

"I don't care how charming you are, Pablo," Rosa called out toward the den just before she stepped into the kitchen. "You are not getting any more ice cream tonight."

Sofia and Tornado padded in behind her.

Rosa glanced in Vanessa's direction and gave her a sympathetic smile. "You've been through a lot, honey." She put her ice-cream bowls and spoons in the dishwasher. "And you promised me you'd go to bed early. Get some rest."

"I remember." Exhaustion had been tugging at her since early afternoon.

Rosa set two prescription bottles and a glass of water in front of her.

Vanessa took the pills. Then she stood and summoning up what little bit of strength she had left, she put on her tough lawyer face and turned to Levi. "I may be moving a little bit slower right now, but I *will* pick up speed and jump right back into the heart of the investigation into my father's murder. And we're going to find this man who thinks he's going to kill me."

Levi also stood. And if Vanessa wasn't mistaken, there was a hint of admiration in his dark brown eyes. "I would expect no less," he said.

Levi's phone alarm chimed early the next morning. He'd set it to wake him well before sunrise. There was a long day ahead of him.

He opened the door of his bedroom, located on the first floor of the ranch house across from the den, and saw light spilling out into the hallway from the kitchen. No surprise. Everybody here lived by rancher's hours. He knew the routine. He'd grown up with it.

The sound and rich scent of gurgling coffee drew him to the kitchen. He also smelled something sugary and delicious baking.

Vanessa sat at the kitchen table with an open laptop in front of her and her right hand wrapped around a thick blue mug half-full of black coffee.

"Morning," Pablo called out from beside the stove, where he'd just pulled out a pan of cinnamon rolls and set them on the stovetop. That was what Levi had smelled.

"Hi." Vanessa turned to him. She had on gray sweatpants and a University of Nevada, Las Vegas, sweatshirt. Her platinum curly hair was piled up on her head, held in place by a rhinestone-encrusted clip. And she wore glasses. It took him a moment to realize he was staring at her.

And another moment to realize she'd been staring right back at him.

"How do you take your coffee?" Pablo asked.

"Cream and sugar," Levi answered, silently thanking the man for giving him a reason to look away from Vanessa as he walked over to take the mug from Pablo's hand.

He took a sip and reminded himself that he was here to protect Vanessa. Yes, she was an attractive woman. But right now she was in a vulnerable situation and there was no way he would act on his attraction to her.

Even if she was a fascinating combination of flashy and humble. Intelligent and fun. Compassionate and driven.

And she looked very cute first thing in the morning.

Of course, he'd noticed that her gaze lingered on him sometimes. But if she thought she was attracted to him, it was likely because she saw him as her rescuer. Or she thought of him as heroic because of the uniform and the badge, despite the fact that he'd made it abundantly clear he was no hero.

"Sit down," Pablo commanded, rattling around in the cabinet for some plates. "Rosa and Sam are out checking on the animals. Should be back any minute."

Levi put his hand on the back of a chair and started to pull it out from the table. Then he realized it was occupied by Sofia, the old calico. She lifted her head and blinked, but made no move to jump down. He reached down and scratched her head.

"That's her chair," Vanessa said. "You'll have to pick another one."

"Okay. Which chair belongs to the gray cat? I want to make sure I don't pick that one, either."

Vanessa laughed. "Tornado is outside following Grandpa around."

Pablo started setting plates with cinnamon rolls on the table and gestured at Vanessa to move her laptop.

"Are you looking at the emails I forwarded to you?" Levi asked.

"No, this is stuff from work. I finally told my boss I'm going to have to be here for a while longer. When I told him why, including the fact that I'd been shot, he was sympathetic. And then he sent me some work I can do from here."

"I don't know why you can't just sit around and rest," Pablo grumbled.

"Look who's talking," Vanessa shot back. "You got up in the middle of the night to make these." She gestured with her fork at the cinnamon roll in front of her. Then she turned to Levi. "Go ahead and start eating. Grandpa and Rosa wouldn't want us to wait."

Levi tasted his cinnamon roll and it was as delicious and as buttery as it smelled. He nodded at Pablo. "This is excellent."

Pablo nodded back. "I know."

There wasn't much more talking until the cinnamon rolls had been eaten.

When he was finished, Levi stood and took his dishes to the sink. "Thank you, Pablo. I could eat another one, but I need to get to work."

Vanessa stood and walked with him to the door. "Tomorrow I'll be ready to get back out and work with you on my dad's case."

Levi glanced toward her shoulder. "There's no reason to rush things."

"Yeah, I think there is. For the first time in two *decades*, there's new information." The small smile she offered him was dazzling and he couldn't look away. "I don't want Dad's case to go cold again," she said.

He didn't want it to go cold, either. And he also knew that she would not be safe again until the case was solved.

"You know that Ramirez and I are still working it. *And* looking at forensics and doing everything we can to figure out who is after you."

"Marv Burke never told the police about the fight on the mesa, but he told me. The original prime suspect, Kenny Goren, wasn't willing to talk to you in his shop, but he was willing to talk to *me*. From the beginning, I thought people who wouldn't talk to the cops might talk to me and I was right. There might be more people who will talk to me. Or maybe if you bring someone into the station to talk to them, I might recognize their voice, the way they walk, something that will tell me they are the man who chased me on the mesa. Or maybe it will trigger a memory of someone I saw at the Fargo Hotel." She jutted out her chin. "You *need* my help."

"Things have changed," Levi said, not wanting to take the confidence out of her smile but needing to speak the truth. "Someone hurt you to scare you away. Twice. And now, after firing all those shots at you, I think it's pretty obvious they're trying to *kill* you."

"And I'm terrified. But sometimes the only way out of something is to go through it. I can't hide here forever. Whoever is after me could kill me just as easily in Vegas if I packed it all in and went back there. We can't lose momentum in finding my dad's murderer."

Levi wanted to tell her no. That staying here, safe and protected for as long as it took, was the only possible option. But ultimately it wasn't his call. She was her own woman. "Ramirez and I are meeting with Chief Haskell this morning to talk about both of your cases. I'll let you know what happens."

"All right."

"And make sure you lock the door behind me."

He arrived at the police station and between one thing and another, it was noon before Chief Haskell was finally available to meet with Levi and Ramirez. They ordered pizza and ate it in one of the offices while reviewing the information they had and making plans to follow up on some of the leads they'd developed.

"The situation is heating up in a way that worries me," the chief said. "The first two attacks on Vanessa were specific and targeted. The shooting on the ranch is a different story." He took a sip of his soda. "Anybody could have gotten hurt. Or killed. Whoever is doing this has gone from brazen to reckless."

"And we still don't know for certain whether there was a second shooter," Ramirez mused aloud. "We only know for certain that two weapons were fired. And the shots came from different directions, but the shooter could have just moved around. The points of origin weren't that far apart." She glanced at Levi. "Maybe our perp is getting more sophisticated and he's intentionally doing things to throw off our investigation. The weapons in the first two attacks were whatever was on hand. For the shooting, he planned ahead and brought his gun. Two guns. He's taking this more seriously now."

The chief leaned forward in his chair and set his cup down on the conference table. "We need to get a bigger team together and go after the perp attacking Vanessa with everything we've got. And we need to be high-profile about it. Make him feel the pressure. Otherwise, he'll think he's got us stymied. And that will just make him bolder."

Levi relayed his conversation with Vanessa,

along with his own opinion that it was too dangerous for her to continue to be involved in the investigations. He felt guilty, like he was betraying her. But it was honestly what he thought and how he felt.

The chief rubbed his hand over his bald head, as he tended to do when he was thinking something through, and tilted his head back to look at the ceiling. Then he took a deep breath and dropped his gaze back to Levi. "You told me when we started this that she was safer investigating her father's murder alongside us, because otherwise she'd investigate on her own. Things have changed since then and now she's deep into some very serious danger. Do you still think if she isn't allowed to work alongside us, she'll investigate on her own?"

A chill passed through Levi's body as he realized the answer. "I think she might."

"Then let her do what she can to help. And stick close to make sure nothing happens to her. We need to get this current would-be killer off the streets, fast. And if continuing to dig into the past will help us do it, then that's what we'll do."

NINE

"How did you find out Trent O'Connell was back in town?" Vanessa turned in the passenger seat of Levi's police SUV to look at him while she waited for an answer.

They were driving up to the top of Morgan Mesa. A spring shower had barreled through the area an hour ago and water still dripped from the bright green needles on the pine trees that lined the road.

"Robert O'Connell called me. Said his son was back from his business trip and that he knew I wanted to talk to him. So they invited me to come up to their ranch for a visit."

Vanessa brushed her hair out of her eyes. "Do they know I'm coming?"

"I didn't tell them." He glanced over at her. "Like I told your grandfather, I'm being as careful as I can when you're out with me. There's no sense in announcing your whereabouts to anyone. And if you ever decide you want to hole up somewhere and not come out again until it's safe, I'm one hundred percent fine with that, too."

Grandpa had been pretty surly when Levi returned to the ranch late this morning to pick her up. Vanessa had done her best to reassure Sam and remind him that the only way to bring this nightmare to an end was by doing everything possible to identify the murderer who was apparently behind it all. She had to do everything she could to make that happen.

The road rose upward and wound around a curve to reveal a break in the trees. She could see heavy gray clouds hovering over rusty-colored mesas and tree-covered mountains in the distance.

Northern Nevada was beautiful country. But it could be rough, inhospitable country, too. Vanessa came from tough people. "When you get knocked down, you get back up," she said softly.

From the corner of her eye, she saw Levi nod once. "Agreed."

He clearly had something on his mind, so for the time being she let her gaze linger on the surrounding scenery while she listened to the police radio. Most of the transmissions were about mundane things. Somebody got pulled over for expired license tags. There was a deer trapped in the playground equipment at an elementary school in town. A welfare check request had been called in by someone who lived over in Carson City and was worried about his uncle.

At any moment, something could happen to make this day—or any day—the absolute worst day of someone's life. Or their last one. It was funny how things turned out. She'd gone through the horror of learning she'd never see her beloved dad again. And then the tumultuous and terrifying experience of those years living with her stepfather. And now look what she did for a living. As a defense attorney, she often dealt with people having one terrible day after another.

She'd told herself more than once that was why she'd gone through those experiences. So she could help others.

She glanced over at Levi, trying to be subtle as she watched him. She couldn't help thinking that in a way he'd had similarly tumultuous life experiences. Though in his case he'd been through combat and everything that went along with that. Trying to survive after seemingly random events broke his heart and turned his world on end. And now as a cop, he also often worked with people who were having the worst days of their lives.

It was a strange thing for the two of them to have in common. A very particular way to be of service in a world filled with people who often didn't want to hear about God's unfailing love but who would be willing to take hold of a hand offered in help. And who knew, maybe that one little break in their armor would one day open their minds and hearts wide enough to let faith in. And comfort. And maybe a sense of themselves as having value.

She liked having something in common with him. Something beyond a couple of hopefully temporary investigations.

That thought made her nervous. Because along with this realization was a truth she couldn't hide from herself: she might not just want to be buddies with him. She might want something more from him.

Or not.

Probably not.

The last romantic relationship she'd had ended a year and a half ago. Three months after it officially started. She and the very successful businessman she was seeing were having a nice dinner together. Vanessa had been on the legal defense team for a murder case, which had her thinking about fate and she'd asked her companion, "Do you think the time and the way we pass on are determined before we're even born?"

The response she'd gotten from her date was a mild snort accompanied by an eye roll as he reached for a piece from the appetizer plate they were sharing. "Please, Vanessa," he'd said. "Can we talk about something less depressing?"

Depressing? She'd thought of it as a spiritual question. And spiritual questions were the kind of thing she liked to ponder when she had time to think about something other than work.

She'd apologized for bringing up the topic. Now she regretted the apology. But at the time his annoyed comment had put her in a state where she was emotionally back to being the weird girl in high school whose dad was murdered. Just like she'd been that same "weird girl" in college.

Oh, she'd learned to cover up that awkward feeling and the insecurity that had plagued her. She wore her flashy clothes, got excellent grades and once she'd graduated from law school, she'd quickly earned a reputation for being a "pit bull" of a defense attorney in a courtroom.

But still, there was that part of her that remained fragile and defensive no matter what she did.

In a way, that last date with Bill-the-last-boyfriend had been good for her. Because it brought her to the moment when she accepted that she might just be a different sort of woman. And that she didn't need to adjust her way of looking at life to fit someone else's definition of *normal*.

She sighed, bringing her thoughts back to the present and focusing on the shafts of sunlight breaking through the clouds in the distance. Not everyone was meant to have a romantic life. Maybe she was part of that group.

She had family. She had friends. A career. There was a lot to be grateful for.

"Do you think the exact time and way we pass on is already planned out before we're even born?" she asked Levi, and then waited for an indication of annoyance or maybe a shallow, flippant response.

He didn't answer right away. "I don't have a specific answer for that. I wonder about it, too. I place my faith in a loving God who counts every soul as precious," he finally said, glancing at her. “Your dad’s life and death mattered. Your dad mattered.” He turned his gaze back to the road in front of them.

“I saw a lot of death when I served overseas,” he continued, his voice starting to sound a little hoarse. “When I tried to figure out a good reason for why the people I knew and loved suffered, I couldn’t come up with one. Going in mental circles, trying to understand exactly where God’s grace intersected with man’s free will didn’t help. Neither did drinking. The only thing that helps me with that question is to trust God and to press on in faith.”

Vanessa felt a hard knot rise up in her throat and tears began to pool in her eyes. She’d heard variations of what Levi had just said before. But for some reason, hearing them right now felt soothing and freeing in a way they hadn’t before. They felt like a healing touch. *Thank You, Lord.*

She looked over at Levi. He still had that calm, unruffled expression he wore on his face most of the time.

He glanced in her direction. “What’s the matter?” He took his foot off the accelerator and the SUV slowed down.

It wasn’t until she saw the concern on his face that she realized she was crying. “I’m fine." Vanessa hurriedly wiped her eyes with the backs of her hands.

He pulled the SUV over onto the muddy shoulder of the road.

"Why are you stopping?" She turned to look him in the eye, then impatiently waved her hand toward the blacktop. "Let's keep going."

"You've been through a lot," he said. "Let me take you back—"

"I had a moment," she admitted, but she wasn't about to apologize for it. Yes, her emotions might be all over the place. But she knew where she placed her faith. "I'm fine now. And I'm looking forward to talking to Trent O'Connell." She intentionally put on the game face she used in the courtroom. But the strength she felt was real. "I want to keep the investigation moving. I want *answers*."

His gaze settled on her face for a few seconds. He was trying to get a read on her. Figure out if she really could handle an interview at the O'Connell ranch.

She knew she could.

As had been the case before, more than once, she saw the depths of strength and compassion in his eyes.

After a moment, the corner of his mouth

lifted in a slight smile. "*We* want answers from Trent O'Connell. Try not to scare him."

She raised her eyebrows as if thinking it over. "I'm not promising anything."

Levi pulled the SUV back onto the road and twenty minutes later, they were on the top of Morgan Mesa and making the turn onto the O'Connell ranch property. When they knocked on the door of the house, Robert answered. "Welcome," he said, nodding a greeting at Levi and then smiling at Vanessa. "Come on back. My son is in the study."

Trent O'Connell sat in the leather-covered executive chair behind the heavy oak desk in the same room where they'd originally spoken to Robert. His sandy blond hair was parted on the side and combed over. He had to be in his early forties at least, but his slightly ruddy cheeks made him look younger. He got to his feet and offered a bland, tired-looking smile. Dressed in tan slacks and a burgundy polo shirt, he looked more like a businessman than a cowboy.

Once the introductions were out of the way and everyone was seated, Levi started a general conversation with Trent. Vanessa knew about questioning people and figured he'd eventually work his way to the pointed questions he really wanted to ask.

Vanessa had already taken notice of Trent's stance and the way he moved. Now she paid as much attention to the sound of his voice as she did to the meaning of his words, trying to determine if he could be the thug who'd chased her on the mesa.

But nothing about him seemed particularly familiar.

"We're taking a second look at some of the information gathered during the original investigation into Josh Ford's murder," Levi said to Trent. "Also I've got some questions regarding the more recent attacks on Vanessa."

"I don't know how I can help," Trent said. "But ask me whatever you'd like."

"According to the case notes, you left town right about the time Josh Ford was murdered," Levi said. "Where did you go?"

"Are you accusing me of something?" Trent's bland smile vanished and his eyes narrowed.

"Maybe we need to continue this with a lawyer present," Robert said. Then he glanced at Vanessa. "A lawyer other than you, of course."

Vanessa smiled at him as though he'd made a good joke and it seemed to break the tension.

Trent's eyes were no longer narrowed and

his smile had returned. Maybe that weak joke really had eased the tension in the room. Or maybe it had just given him time to pull himself together and hide his defensive emotions.

"It's all right, Dad," Trent said. "I've got nothing to hide. I started college in California at that time. Sacramento State."

If that were true, it could easily be verified.

"Do you have any theories about who murdered Josh?" Levi asked.

"The police had Kenny Goren in custody. That loser drank through his money as fast as he could. He was always broke. He and Josh never got along. Why don't you talk to him?"

"He told us to talk to you," Levi said mildly.

"Well, he'd be my main suspect," Trent responded.

"Did Marv Burke hang around here back during that time?" Vanessa asked. It was possible Marv had given them the clue about seeing the two men fighting in an attempt to make himself look innocent.

"Marv never worked here," Robert interjected.

"But he was an entrepreneur way back before he bought his gas station," Trent added. "He used to come out here to sell weed to workers, especially the seasonal employees who didn't already have a supplier."

Robert gave his son a startled look. Trent shrugged in return.

"What about more recently?" Levi asked. "Trent, I'm sure your father told you about the attack on Vanessa on the grounds of the old Heaton homestead eleven days ago. Where have you been from that time until now?"

"Traveling for work," Trent answered.

"Where, exactly?"

He hesitated, then crossed his arms over his chest. "Now I'm really thinking I might need an attorney. Do you think I was the attacker on the mesa?"

"We're just trying to clear as many people as possible so we can focus on substantial suspects," Levi said.

"I was in Las Vegas," Trent said. "Then Los Angeles."

"You traveled by plane?"

"No. I drove. And I'm still tired from the trip. But my dad wanted me to talk to you right away. Now I have."

Vanessa had the distinct impression he was done talking to them.

Levi glanced at her and raised his eyebrows marginally as if asking if she had any more questions. She shook her head slightly and they both got to their feet. They said their goodbyes and Robert saw them out.

"So what do you think?" Vanessa asked as they walked across the crushed-rock driveway to the SUV.

"I'm becoming more convinced there was something going on up here on the O'Connell ranch twenty years ago. Something that involved your dad, Robert, Trent, Marv and Kenny Goren. And that's why your father was murdered."

"Something going on? Like what?" Vanessa asked.

"I don't know."

She rubbed her hands over her arms, trying to ward off a sudden chill. "So you think I've already come face-to-face with the man who chased me at the Heaton house and who's been terrorizing me ever since? That I've been talking to him without realizing it?"

"Maybe. Or maybe someone else is responsible for the attacks on you. Somebody who isn't on our suspect list yet. And he'll likely make another attempt on your life soon."

"How do you feel about hitting the drive-through at a coffee stand before we head back down the mesa?" Vanessa asked Levi after they left the O'Connell ranch.

He tapped the steering wheel with his thumbs as he followed the road through what passed for downtown Morgan Mesa. "You're not going to like my answer."

"It can't be that dangerous to get a cup of coffee."

"For one thing, I want to get some distance between you and this mesa." That conversation with the O'Connells had his mind working overtime, thinking of possible reasons why there could have been bad blood between Josh Ford, Trent and Robert O'Connell, Marv Burke and Kenny Goren twenty years ago. And why one of them would want to silence Vanessa.

Or possibly two of them wanted her dead. Working with that theory complicated things.

"We know I could be targeted anywhere," she said with a flat tone that made Levi think bitterness was rapidly becoming her dominant mood. All things considered, he could hardly blame her. "And my head is pounding."

"Sorry. Waiting outside a drive-through window or inside a shop for a coffee would make me feel like we were sitting ducks and that's not something I can live with. When we get back to the ranch, I'll brew you all the coffee you want."

"All right."

He glanced over and she was looking in the side-view mirror. Good. He wanted her vigilant. Even if keeping her on edge made his gut twist a little. He knew what it was like to fear for your life and desperately want a break from that tension. But this was not the time for that.

Like her, he checked his mirrors to see if anyone was following them. Problem was he didn't know exactly what he was looking for. There were other vehicles on the road, but he couldn't see into all of them. Any one of his suspects could be following them just a couple of vehicles back. Or for all he knew, the added unidentified suspect that he'd theorized could exist might be right behind them.

Finally, he passed the small café at the end of the business district. The speed limit increased here and Levi hit the gas. The sooner he got Vanessa back to the Silver Horse, the better he'd feel.

They were halfway down the mesa, each lost in their own thoughts, when Levi's phone rang. He answered with the hands-free device.

"Levi, where are you?" It was Chief Haskell.

"We just finished talking with the O'Connells and we're heading back to the house."

"Vanessa's with you?" the chief asked.

"Yes."

There was a pause and Levi could hear phones ringing, people talking and all the familiar sounds of the police department squad room. The chief was discussing something with somebody else. Levi recognized the voices of the two officers who'd been assigned part of his caseload so he could focus on Vanessa and her dad's cold case.

"Sommers and Tempe believe they've got a couple of leads on those commercial burglaries you were investigating. I need you to come down to the station and look at some video and pictures they've got and run some names by you. Get your take on a couple of ideas."

Levi glanced over at Vanessa. "You okay with going into town?" he asked. "Or do you want me to take you back to the ranch?"

"I'll go," she said.

They were nearly at the bottom of the mesa. "Be there in twenty," Levi said to the chief.

Once they reached the station, Levi made a fresh pot of coffee in the breakroom, poured some for Vanessa and himself and then got her settled in one of the small conference rooms on the edge of the main floor where he could see her through the glass. He knew it was ridiculous for him to worry about her safety in a police station, but being able to glance over at her now and then while he worked with the detectives made him feel better.

There were a couple of times when he looked over she was talking on her phone with someone, and he found himself wondering about her private life. Did she go out with friends much? Was she a workaholic like he tended to be? What did she do when she wanted to unwind and have fun?

He looked at all the new evidence the detectives had, discussed theories and answered their questions. By the time they were finished, he had a good feeling about the case. It looked like it was going to get wrapped up very soon.

When Levi stepped outside with Vanessa to head back to the ranch, it was well past sunset and a full moon was out. One of his favorite things about Torchlight was that the downtown area where the police department headquarters was located still had an old Western historical look about it. Everything from the streetlight fixtures to the storefronts to the exterior of the Fargo Hotel spoke of a community that appreciated its heritage. And it all looked especially romantic in the moonlight.

Now, that was a ridiculous thought. He laughed at himself and shook his head.

"What?" Vanessa asked.

"Nothing." He needed to keep his thoughts focused on the street in front of them as they walked to his SUV. And on the alleyways and on anybody passing by on the sidewalk. All places where danger could come at them unexpectedly.

He glanced several times at his mirrors as they left town, trying to see if anybody was following them. He also tried making conversation with Vanessa. She was polite, but it was clear she had something on her mind and wanted to be left alone. Maybe she was tired.

They passed beneath the tall streetlights at the highway's intersection, with the road up to the mesa. Just a few more miles beyond it and they'd be at the ranch where Vanessa could get some rest.

He heard a noise outside the vehicle on the passenger side and then suddenly something was moving toward them down the hillside. In the darkness, he could barely see what it was, but it looked like a falling tree. "Hold on!" he hollered to Vanessa as he yanked the steering wheel hard to the left.

He was too late. There was already another tree in front of them lying across the road. The SUV skidded as he tried to avoid crashing into it and the rear of the vehicle started swinging around to the front.

He heard Vanessa scream as he threw his arm out in front of her to protect her and the SUV slammed into the fallen tree and began to roll over onto its side. The SUV's airbags deployed explosively at the same time that the tree branches jammed into the front and passenger-side windows, cracking the safety glass.

The tree was massive and heavy and didn't move much as the SUV smashed into it. The thick branches offered just enough cushioning that the SUV didn't completely roll onto its side. The branches kept it propped up, but it felt like it would tip over at any minute.

Seconds later, the tree rolling down the hill crashed to the ground behind them.

"You all right?" Levi asked when the sickening sliding and tipping motion of the SUV finally stopped. He looked over at Vanessa. In the dim illumination from the instrument panel, he could see her face. Her eyes looked huge.

"I'm all right," she whispered.

"Are you sure?" He quickly unbuckled his seat belt and started to climb over the center console to reach her, to touch her and make sure she wasn't bleeding and nothing was broken.

But as he moved toward her, the SUV began to shift. The passenger side, tilted at an angle, was being kept from crashing to the pavement by the tree branches holding it up. And as he moved toward her and put more weight on those branches, they started to snap.

Not good.

His thoughts ran in a dozen different directions. Was this just some freak accident? Had somebody set up an ambush? Was the psychopath intent on murdering Vanessa creeping up on them at this very minute, determined to fire a final bullet into her?

It took him a moment to realize she'd said something to him. She was asking if he was okay.

"I'm fine," he said. The bumps and bruises he'd just taken meant nothing to him. Protecting Vanessa meant everything.

Slowly, cautiously, limiting his movement as much as possible, he reached for the mic on his radio and called for help. But he couldn't just stay there and wait for help to arrive. Not only might Vanessa's stalker be closing in on them, but they had oncoming traffic to worry about. Fortunately, this section of highway was fairly quiet at this time of night. But they were in the middle of the road. Anyone coming from either direction, if they weren't paying attention, would plow right into them.

Levi reached over and unfastened Vanessa's seat belt. There was no way she was getting out through her door. It was pressed into the fallen tree and trying to get out that way could cause the SUV to fall on top of her.

Levi checked to make certain his pistol was still at his side. He opened his door. Then he turned to Vanessa and reached both of his hands out to her and she clasped them.

"I'm going to pull on your hands and at the same time I want you to climb out of your seat, over the console, over my seat and jump outside with me. Do you understand what I'm saying?"

She nodded. "Yes."

He squeezed her hands. "Okay, *now*!"

He pulled hard, she jumped out of her seat and over like a champ. He pulled her free just as the SUV started shifting again. The branches broke with loud cracks and the SUV slammed down hard on the pavement on the passenger side.

Levi didn't realize he had her wrapped tightly in his arms until he felt her heart beating against his chest.

For a second, he felt relief at surviving the crash and getting Vanessa out of there.

But they were standing on the highway, unprotected, and they had to move.

Hating to do it, he unwrapped his arms from around her, then clasped her hand. With the other hand, he drew his pistol. He gestured toward the side of the highway and a cluster of trees. "We need to take cover."

She nodded her understanding.

Levi started moving and prayed they'd be safe until help arrived.

TEN

Vanessa sat alone in Sergeant Ramirez's patrol car. She was in the front seat, where warm air from the vent in front of her blew over the surface of her skin. But she was still cold.

Cops had quickly responded to Levi's call for help after the crash. He had chosen to stay on scene, directing the efforts in the middle of the action. But he wanted Vanessa safely tucked away in the patrol car and she was fine with that. She was scared. And numb, if it was possible to be both at the same time. Most likely she was in shock.

And she was worried about Levi. She watched him on the blocked-off section of highway, walking and talking with the traffic-incident investigators.

Vanessa wasn't the only one who should be careful. Levi was so closely associated with protecting her and reopening the investigation into her dad's murder that he'd likely made himself a target for whoever was out to silence her.

Bright white light from a fire engine's headlights shone across the road and off to the side, where the fallen trees that could have triggered a fatal accident lay.

There was no mistaking the significance of the smooth bottom edge of both tree trunks.

Those trees had not fallen on their own. They'd been deliberately cut down.

The perfect timing of their fall demonstrated an impressive skill, but not a completely unusual one in northern Nevada. Foresters, ranchers and wildlands firefighters among others needed to know how to control the fall of a tree. They'd do that by making a series of small cuts into the trunk of the tree before making the final cut that sent it crashing downward. And, in this case, rolling onto the highway.

The setup and timing had been nearly perfect enough to trigger a fatal crash.

Close, but not close enough. She blew out a shallow breath, her lungs still tight with fear, and whispered a prayer of thanks.

In the light from the emergency vehicles, she could see Levi put his phone up to his ear and then tilt his head back to look up at the hillside where the fallen trees had come from. He nodded a couple of times, disconnected the call and then waved to Sergeant Ramirez. Together, he and Ramirez walked over to the car where Vanessa sat.

She opened the passenger door as they approached, intending to get out, but Levi gestured for her to close the door and roll down her window instead.

"You still doing all right?" he asked her, concern in his eyes. He had a few small cuts and scrapes on his face. She could feel that she had some of her own, too. "I can radio for an ambulance to come out here. Have you checked out, just to make sure you're okay."

Vanessa shook her head. "I'm fine." The pressure of the seat belt holding her in place had pressed down on her shoulder near the spot where the bullet had grazed her and she'd yelped in pain as the SUV slid and then tilted. But the wound had not been reopened, she'd already checked for that. And she hadn't done anything to her head other than the jolt against the headrest when the SUV finally came to a stop.

"I saw you talking on your phone," Ramirez said. She looked inquiringly at Levi. "What have you learned?" The sergeant had been the first to arrive on the scene. Clearly anxious to track down whoever was responsible for this attack, she tapped her booted foot impatiently.

Levi pointed up the side of the hill toward the power lines that led off in the direction of the mesa. "I was talking to the guys we've got looking around up there. They say there's an access road for the power company to use. The road's actually more of a narrow path, barely wide enough for a pickup truck."

"There must be signs that someone was just up there," Ramirez said.

Levi nodded. "Some freshly snapped twigs. Tire tracks in the mud. The officers are going to stay until somebody can get up there to take impressions of the tire tracks and look for any other evidence. Realistically, they probably won't get much done before daylight."

"It had to be Trent O'Connell," Vanessa said. "Can't you go arrest him? Our questions obviously annoyed him. He was defensive. He probably figured we knew more than we actually do and that we were closing in on him. He could have followed us after we left the ranch. Saw we made the turn toward Torchlight. He knew we'd have to pass by this point eventually to get back to the ranch."

Ramirez narrowed her eyes and nodded thoughtfully. She turned to Levi. "I'll go get him."

"Whoa," Levi said, putting a staying hand on her arm.

Vanessa was barely listening to them now. Burning with fury, she wondered if she'd spent twenty minutes earlier this evening chatting with the man who'd murdered her father.

"I know how you feel," Levi said to Ramirez. "I want to get somebody locked up for this, too. And I'd like to do it tonight. But that's not likely to happen. Jumping to conclusions isn't the way the justice system functions. You know that." He turned to Vanessa. "*We* know that."

"So get a search warrant," Vanessa snapped, giving in to her emotions at the moment and asking for what she wanted to have happen rather than what she logically knew could happen. "Go back up to the O'Connell ranch and look for a chainsaw and a truck that might have recently driven along that access road up there." She waved toward the top of the hill.

"I know how to do my job," Levi replied evenly. "And no judge is going to think a recent conversation with Trent O'Connell where he got annoyed with us provides enough probable cause for a search warrant."

For a moment, she just stared at him. Furious. Why wouldn't he get moving? Go arrest the man who had killed her father?

And then the wave of frustration and anger subsided. Because, of course, she knew he was right. And she knew how to do her job as a defense attorney, too. If they didn't follow proper procedures or didn't collect enough solid evidence to build a case, the murderer could potentially walk free.

That could *not* happen.

She took a deep breath and blew it out.

Get it together. Emotions were notoriously unreliable. Particularly in matters involving the justice system.

It was entirely possible that what seemed like the obvious truth to her right now could be something else. Maybe someone wanted to make Trent O'Connell look guilty. She could think of at least two people who might be motivated to do that. Namely, their two other suspects, Kenny Goren and Marv Burke. Any one of them could have followed Vanessa and Levi from the time they left the O'Connell ranch.

"I've talked to Chief Haskell a couple of times since we've been out here," Levi said.

"He's dispatching officers to wait outside the homes of Kenny Goren and Marv Burke, as well as the O'Connells. They'll be keeping an eye on things. Looking to see if anything obvious happens tonight that might connect them to what happened here on the highway."

"Are you going to have the officers knock on their doors and talk to them?" Vanessa asked.

"When it's time for that, I'll talk to them myself." Levi turned to Ramirez. "I want to get back to the station and talk to the chief in person. Let me borrow your patrol car."

"All right." She rested her hands on her hips and squared her shoulders. "I'll stay until everything's done and I can clear the scene." She glanced toward the fire engine. "Maybe I'll get a ride back to the station on that."

"Just make sure you keep your guard up while you're out here," Levi warned her. "Whoever did this could be hanging around, watching. They might decide to fire a shot at you just to make some kind of point."

"I'll be careful," she said.

Levi slid into the vehicle and buckled up.

"Hey, you take care of my car," Ramirez called out to him. "Don't smash it up like you did your poor SUV over here."

"Yeah, yeah." Levi waved her away with a faint smile on his face. "You just go do your job."

Vanessa wasn't happy to admit it to herself, but just having Levi in the car with her and sitting beside her made her feel better. Not just safer because there was a cop a few inches away from her. But better. A little bit stronger. *Happier*, even, which was absurd given the experience they'd just survived.

Still. Her response to him was something she'd have to sort out eventually. But not now.

"Did you call your grandpa while you were waiting here in the car to tell him what happened?" Levi asked.

That was something she really didn't want to do.

"Not yet," she said. They weren't far from the turnoff to the ranch house. But the house was far enough back from the highway that it was likely no one had heard the sirens blaring when Ramirez and the other emergency responders had arrived.

Levi rubbed his hand over his jaw. "Where do you want me to take you?"

What did he mean? She'd assumed he was going to take her back to the ranch. "What are my options?"

"I can take you home. To the ranch. You've

been through a lot and you're tired, and I understand that. But I can't do my job from there. And right now I don't want you going anywhere without me."

"Are you saying you want me to go with you back to the police station?"

"Yes. I know it could be a long night. But I want to be at the station if any of the officers report seeing something suspicious at the home of one of our suspects. I could have an officer staged at the ranch for your protection if you want to go there. But if there's an incident in this area that needs an immediate response—a car accident, a prowler, whatever—that officer will be dispatched to respond. Which would leave you unprotected. The person behind all of this might even call in a fake report for that exact reason."

Vanessa had already drawn enough danger to the ranch. The last thing she wanted to do was bring even more.

And really, she was tired of this. Tired of the fear. Tired of her dad's murder being unresolved. The attacks on her and the injuries to her poor body. Tired of *all* of it.

Levi was offering her a chance to potentially be at the center of the action when the police captured whoever was attacking her. And maybe even when they brought her dad's murderer to justice.

"I'm fine with going to the police station with you," she said.

"Thank you." He shifted the car into gear and turned it around so they were heading toward Torchlight instead of the ranch.

"But now I *really* want some coffee," she said.

He didn't respond. They were on a straight stretch of highway and Levi's attention was focused on the dark road ahead. And apparently his own thoughts, as well. Vanessa glanced over at the speedometer. They were moving pretty fast.

Maybe the investigation was finally heading toward a conclusion. Which would be good in the long run. But at the moment that thought wasn't exactly comforting.

"Stay where you are for right now," Chief Haskell said toward the speaker on his desk phone. "Call if you see any activity. I'll check in with you in an hour." He glanced at Levi. "Or Lieutenant Hawk will check in with you." He disconnected the call.

Levi stood by the chief's desk, frustrated to hear that the officer outside the O'Connell ranch hadn't seen anything useful. Like maybe Trent pulling a chainsaw from the back of a tree-scratched pickup truck. That could get things wrapped up pretty quick.

He shook off the thought. Hadn't he been the one warning Vanessa and Ramirez about getting tunnel vision barely more than an hour ago?

"What have you heard from the officers watching Marv Burke and Kenny Goren?" Levi asked the chief.

"Nothing yet. We've got to give them time to get into place." The chief leaned back in his chair and rubbed his hand over his head. "I know you're anxious and hoping for a break in the case tonight, but it might not happen. It could take days or weeks. Or it could take a whole lot longer."

The chief shifted his attention toward the pane of glass that separated his office from the squad room and Levi followed his gaze.

Vanessa sat in Levi's chair at his desk. She held her phone up to her ear with one hand while crumpling a paper coffee cup in the other and then tossing it into a nearby trash can. Then she disconnected the call.

Levi had tried to get her to settle in someplace more comfortable. There was a breakroom with a cushioned sofa and a TV on the other side of the building, but she'd said for now she wanted to stay in the squad room. In case she was needed.

"It's almost seven," the chief said. "Has she eaten dinner?"

Guilt took a punch at Levi's gut. He'd convinced her to come to the station with him so he'd be sure she was safe. But she needed more than just security. He should have been taking care of her. Instead, he was so focused on the chase for the criminal who was tormenting her that he'd dropped the ball on that.

"I'll order sandwiches for everybody on shift right now," the chief said. "And then I'm heading home. If you're planning on staying until morning, I'll have the officers watching our suspects tonight check in with you. I'll be available by phone."

Levi walked out into the squad room and pulled out the empty chair at Ramirez's desk so he was sitting across from Vanessa. "Dinner will be here in a few minutes," he said.

She gave him a blank look, like food was the last thing on her mind. Then she gestured toward her phone lying on his desk. "Grandpa called. Our accident was on the news. Including the fact that the tree was intentionally cut down in order to cause us to crash."

Levi stared at her for a moment, desperate to say the right words to make her feel better but having no clue what those words might be. "Well, since your grandpa talked to you, he knows you're fine," he finally said.

"Yeah. But he doesn't sound so great."

"He was upset?" Levi couldn't blame him for that. But maybe she meant he'd lost his temper.

"He sounded tired," Vanessa said, her voice husky. "I'm worried he's going to have a heart attack or maybe a stroke." Tears formed in the corners of her eyes. "The last few months have already been hard on him with my grandmother passing away. All of this stuff happening to me is making things a lot worse for him."

Levi got up, walked around the desks and then pulled over a chair so that he could sit beside her. He wrapped an arm around her shoulder and pulled her close against him. Maybe it wasn't the most professional thing to do, but it felt right. "Your grandpa's a tough old cowboy," Levi said. "He'll hang on tight no matter how rough the ride gets."

Vanessa sniffed loudly. She turned her face in his direction and Levi could feel the warmth of her breath passing over his skin as she exhaled. After a few moments of sitting quietly together, he was aware of her shoulder muscles beginning to relax. Despite the sadness of the situation, he felt a sense of accomplishment knowing he'd eased her burdens a little. Even if it was just for the moment.

Vanessa pulled slightly away and her gaze met his. There was no missing the sorrow in her eyes. This chase for the bad guys was tied to horrible memories for her. Any sense of triumph he felt at capturing the criminals needed to be tempered by that fact. What might feel like cause for celebration for law enforcement would likely be a bittersweet moment for her. Because when they arrested someone, she'd see the face of her father's killer.

Just before the food arrived, Levi checked in with the officer watching the O'Connell ranch. Unfortunately, he hadn't seen any movement at all. "Nobody going in or out of the place," he'd reported. "Everything's quiet up here."

Shortly after, the other officer up on the mesa, the one assigned to watch Marv Burke, called in to report he'd learned Marv was working at his gas station.

"Go into the gas station's convenience store and buy a soda," Levi told him. "Try to chat with Marv. Be relaxed about it, like you just happened to be in the neighborhood doing some routine patrolling, don't make it seem like he's a suspect for anything. See if he seems nervous or edgy. Or if he has recent cuts or scratches that he could have gotten by tromping out into the forest and cutting down a couple of trees."

"Maybe he'll smell like pine resin," the officer joked.

"Good point," Levi said flatly, not much in the mood for humor. "Tell me if he does."

Twenty minutes later that same officer called back. "I talked to Marv," he reported. "He didn't seem nervous. Didn't look like he'd recently been out in the woods, though he obviously would have had enough time by now to go home and shower and change clothes if he had cut down those trees."

"Park out of sight and keep an eye on him for a little while longer," Levi said and then disconnected.

Ramirez stopped by the station to take her dinner break and grab one of the sandwiches the chief had ordered. She'd been assigned routine patrol for the day and she was just about to wrap up her shift and go home.

Levi got her up to date. "Have you heard

anything from the officer watching Kenny Goren?" she asked.

"I know he reported to the chief when he initially arrived on scene. And that he's positioned at the end of the road where Goren's business and house trailer are located. His directions were to stay out of sight so Goren wouldn't know he was being watched. And to report anybody going onto or leaving the property."

Levi thought about what he'd just said. The layout of Kenny's business, away from the road and surrounded by old cars and piles of junk, meant the officer couldn't know for certain if Kenny was there without making himself visible. He'd have to pull in one end of the semicircular drive and out the other and that would make him very visible.

Apparently, Vanessa had the same thought at the same time. "Are we certain Kenny is sitting quietly at home?" she asked.

No, they weren't.

Levi called the chief.

"Go ahead and have the officer out there check and see if Goren is on the property," Haskell said. "I'd hoped one of our suspects would do something foolish tonight, quickly try to dump evidence or meet up together or *something*, if they didn't know they were being watched. Looks like that's not going to happen. So, yeah. Tell the officer there to go ahead and make contact with him. But keep it subtle. Tell him a business in the area has been burglarized and we want to know if he's had any problems."

Levi passed along the directions to the officer and told him to report back as soon as he had anything.

Then he glanced at Vanessa. She'd unwrapped her sandwich and opened her bag of chips, but it didn't look like she'd actually eaten anything.

"If we catch some action on this case tonight and you can't keep up because you didn't eat and you don't have any energy, don't blame me," he teased.

She rolled her eyes. Then a slight smile lifted the corners of her lips and she reached for a barbecued potato chip. When Levi's phone rang a few minutes later, she was near the bottom of the bag.

"Goren's not in his shop or in his house trailer," the officer at the scene reported. "Doors are unlocked, lights are on, both at the shop and the house. Looks like he left in a hurry."

Levi's heart started to race. Maybe the break

in the case they'd all been hoping and praying for was finally at hand.

"Stand by," he told the officer. He disconnected and immediately called the chief. Vanessa could listen in and hear him report what he'd just learned.

"Have dispatch put out an alert to let us know if anyone sees his car," the chief said. "At the moment, we don't have any reason to arrest him. Tell the officer at Goren's business to canvass the neighborhood and find out if Goren's neighbors heard or saw anything."

Levi talked to dispatch and then called the officer at Goren's property to pass along the chief's directions.

The officer called back again a few minutes later. "People near Goren's place say he tore out of here at high speed about an hour after your crash on the highway."

Levi told the officer to stay put. He disconnected and called the chief to update him. The whole time he spoke to the chief, Levi watched Vanessa. Of course she was listening to every word he said, her expression moving from surprised to thoughtful and then determined.

"You make sure that officer doesn't try to snoop around without permission from Goren or a warrant," she said as soon as Levi disconnected, sounding every bit like the tough lawyer she was. "If it turns out that after all these years my dad's killer really was the suspect the police had their eyes on twenty years ago, I don't want any evidence tossed out because it was obtained illegally."

"Yes, ma'am," Levi replied. And he texted the cop on scene and reminded him to stay with his patrol car for the time being.

A supervisor from dispatch walked over to Levi's desk a half hour later. "A highway patrol officer has Goren pulled over for speeding about thirty miles out of town," she reported. "The patrol officer says he informed Goren the Torchlight Police Department wants to speak with him. Goren's agreed to come back to town. He told the officer he'd head home and come by the station sometime tomorrow to talk."

Energy shot through Levi like an electrical charge. Things were happening. *Finally.* Maybe they would get it all wrapped up tonight. Find out who murdered Josh Ford *and* end the attacks on Vanessa.

He got to his feet and grabbed his jacket from the back of his chair. Then he called out to Ramirez, who'd lingered at the station despite reaching the end of her shift. "Take your patrol car and meet me at Goren's property. I'm going to grab one of the patrol cars parked out back."

He was nearly out the door when he realized Vanessa was right behind him.

"This could be a volatile situation," Levi said, taking a breath and getting his sudden burst of energy under control. "Goren will probably feel cornered when he sees cops at his house and that could make him dangerous."

"You're not leaving me behind," Vanessa said. "The last time he wouldn't talk to you but he spoke to me. That could happen again."

Levi held up his hand. "Wait here. I'll have somebody come get you as soon as we talk to him and know it's safe."

"At that point it'll be too late. If you don't have a reason to arrest him, he'll kick you off his property and you won't get any further information from him. Even if you find a reason to arrest him, you know he'll refuse to talk until he sees a lawyer. I want to be there during that small window of opportunity when he might blurt out something useful."

Levi stared at her for a moment. "All right," he finally said. "I'm not crazy about the idea, but let's go."

A short time later Levi pulled the patrol car

onto Goren's property, drove past the house trailer and up to the shop. The officer who'd been assigned to watch the location was there, along with Ramirez, who'd arrived ahead of them. They waited for a while, and then Goren finally made the turn onto his property. A highway patrol car drove behind him. Apparently, the patrolman had decided to make sure Goren really did make it back to Torchlight.

"Stay behind me the whole time we're here," Levi said to Vanessa as they exited the patrol car.

Goren got out of his own car, glanced at the police cruisers with an expression of distaste, and then walked into his shop. Ramirez and the other officer were right behind him. Through the front window, Levi could see Goren drop down into the chair behind his metal desk. The same place he'd sat when they'd talked to him before.

"How you doing?" Levi asked Goren as he and Vanessa walked inside.

Goren sat stony faced.

There was no way to force the man to talk. But he probably wanted them to leave, so Levi would use that.

"So you heard we wanted to talk to you and you came back. We appreciate that. Actually, the only thing we want from you right now is a timeline of how you spent your day today. Give us that and we'll be on our way," Levi said.

"No," Goren responded.

"Why not?" Levi said, doing his best to keep his body language relaxed and easy and his tone conversational.

Goren looked at Levi, then turned to Vanessa. The hatred in his eyes was so strong the man almost looked like he had a fever. "You're looking for someone to blame." He spat out his words at Vanessa. "And you picked me."

"Why were you running away?" she asked, not looking the slightest bit intimidated.

"I wasn't running away. I was going to Las Vegas to visit a friend."

"But you left without locking everything up or even turning off the lights. You have to know that looks suspicious."

He huffed and kept staring at her, his face turning red with anger. "I saw on the news that somebody had cut down a couple of trees across the highway, probably trying to kill you." He looked out the window and shook his head, and then turned back to Vanessa with an odd, sour grin on his face. "When you showed up before, I knew you were trying to blame me for the attacks on you. And of course, for what happened to your old man. After I saw that story on the news tonight, I knew I had to get out of town. I figured you were going to send the cops after me and I was right."

"Mr. Goren, may we have permission to search your property?" Levi asked.

"It's *Mr.* Goren now?" Goren made a scoffing sound and shook his head. "No. You may not."

"Have you got a chainsaw on your property?" Vanessa asked.

Goren blinked and sighed heavily. Then he glanced around and gestured toward his shop plus all the stuff outside. "I probably do have one here, somewhere. You going to use that to try and pin this car crash thing on me?"

"Did you use a chainsaw earlier this evening to cut down a couple of trees alongside the highway south of town?" Vanessa continued calmly.

"No."

"So why not let the police look around and get yourself cleared as a suspect?"

He sat back in his chair and tapped his foot a few times, scowling. "All right," he finally said. "Go ahead and have a look around the shop and outside. But you stay away from my trailer." He turned and shook his finger at Levi. "You stay out of it. That's my *home*."

Sergeant Ramirez and the patrol officer immediately began searching the shop.

Levi tugged on Vanessa's arm and led her outside. "We need to hurry. Goren could change his mind at any minute. When he showed up here, he was driving a car, but I want to open up these garage doors and see if he's got some kind of vehicle with enough clearance that he could have driven it down that service road to cut down those trees."

They'd just made it to one of the garage doors when Ramirez stepped out of the shop and called to Levi.

"What have you got?" Levi asked, turning and heading back toward her with Vanessa close behind him.

"Nothing." Goren ground out the word when they reached the shop. "She doesn't have anything. And she sure didn't find a chainsaw."

"No chainsaw," Ramirez agreed, a smile on her face. "But I did find this." She held up something and it took Levi a second to realize what he was looking at.

"A hammer." Levi reached for it.

Ramirez nodded. "With the Heaton name engraved on it."

"The hammer missing from the toolshed at the Heaton House," Vanessa said. She turned to Goren. "The hammer you used when you came after me on the mesa."

ELEVEN

"Nobody's trying to pin a murder charge on you," Chief Haskell said to Kenny Goren. "All we're talking about right now are the attacks on Ms. Ford over the last three weeks."

Levi, the chief and Goren were in a small interrogation room at the Torchlight Police Department headquarters. Levi had to admire the chief's interrogation skills. While Goren sat in a plastic chair at the small square metal table, glowering, the chief had literally rolled up his shirtsleeves and was leaning his forearms on the table, talking like he and Goren were best friends.

"I had nothing to do with it," Goren muttered. He wouldn't look the chief or Levi in the eye. Instead, he kept his arms crossed over his chest and stared down at the tabletop.

"What about the hammer?" Levi asked. "How did you end up with that?"

The strategy was for the chief to seem understanding while Levi kept up the accusations. Good cop–bad cop routines were so well-known they were the butt of jokes on TV. Most people might think they were too sophisticated to fall for it, but once an accused person was tired and scared, they became vulnerable to the technique even if they recognized it.

Finally, Goren lifted his gaze. He looked at the chief, and tilted his head slightly. "That hammer don't mean anything," he said, his sneering tone making him sound more like a sullen child than a man in his midforties. "And you ain't gonna find my fingerprints on it."

"So you say." Levi stood and moved to lean against the wall a little closer to Goren, subtly trying to increase the pressure. He took a quick glance toward the camera in the corner of the room up near the ceiling. Vanessa was watching the live feed on the monitor in an adjoining room and he wondered how she was holding up.

Twenty years ago, Goren had been a good suspect for her dad's murder but the officers working the case couldn't get the solid evidence or witnesses needed to press for an arrest and trial. Before this interrogation started, Vanessa had told Levi she was worried that would happen again and Goren would walk away free of any criminal charges.

The chief had been honest when he'd told Goren that right now they were only talking to him about the recent attacks against Vanessa. But he'd also told Levi he would use the threat of murder charges in the death of Josh Ford to pressure Goren to talk if he had to.

At this point, Goren hadn't been arrested and he'd said he was willing to talk without a lawyer present just so he could be cleared as a suspect and go home. But once the questions started, he hadn't been very cooperative. Apparently his habit of not helping the cops was too deeply ingrained.

"You realize we'll be able to track your whereabouts over the last few weeks through your phone," the chief said earnestly, almost sympathetically. "We'll know where you've been, and when."

"That doesn't matter," Goren grumbled. "You won't find anything exciting if you do that."

Maybe he was bluffing. Maybe he'd carried out the attacks without having his phone on him. Or maybe he'd carried an untraceable prepaid phone when doing his dirty work and he'd trashed it immediately afterward.

"We know you've been working with an accomplice," the chief said.

The chief and Levi had talked several times about Vanessa's recounting of the shooting at the Silver Horse Guest Ranch and whether or not there had been two shooters. They still had no proof that there were two people firing the two different guns. But they also didn't have proof that there weren't.

"An accomplice?" Goren's jaw went slack.

Levi crossed his arms over his chest and kept his gaze locked on Goren. Vanessa had to be watching and listening closely, hoping for that break that would take away the fear of immediate danger to her, as well as finally bring closure to the haunting mystery of what had happened to her dad.

A sinister smile slowly crept across Goren's face. "If you had anything on me, you wouldn't be making stuff up."

"Maybe whoever you're working with has you scared," the chief said. "Maybe he's holding something over your head. Something from twenty years ago."

Goren shoved to his feet, glaring at the chief. "Arrest me or let me go."

"All right," Chief Haskell said, also rising to his feet. "Kenny Goren, you're under arrest for breaking and entering, theft and the attempted murder of Vanessa Ford."

"You can't be serious," Goren sputtered.

The handcuffs slapped onto his wrist said otherwise.

When they stepped out of the interrogation room, the chief had an officer take Goren to a holding cell while he started the process of officially filing charges.

Levi went to the conference room where he knew Vanessa would be waiting.

"Well, we've got him locked up," Levi said as soon as he saw her. "He won't be threatening you anymore."

Vanessa nodded. "Good."

She stood with her lower arms crossed just about level with her stomach. Levi could imagine the tension she'd felt as they'd questioned Goren, and the hope that he would tell the story of what had happened to her dad from beginning to end all those years ago.

Levi was disappointed he hadn't been able to give her that.

"You all right?" he asked. Because she didn't look all right. Granted, it had been a very long night. Creeping close to morning. And it had been less than twelve hours since that thug had tried to kill them on the highway. He was probably a pretty sad sight himself.

Her face was pale and her eyes looked a deeper blue than usual, with faint purplish half circles beneath them. She cleared her throat and lifted her chin. "Speaking as a defense attorney, I can tell you that if you can't get a confession, you'll need a lot more evidence that what you have right now to get him convicted in a court of law for what he's done."

"Everyone who is working this case is well aware of that," Levi said, making certain his voice sounded calm and gentle. Vanessa looked vulnerable and fragile despite her determination to protect herself with the armor of her tough lawyer persona. He was afraid it wouldn't take much pressure—of any type—for her to fall apart.

"I appreciate everything all of you are doing," she said, her tone starting out strong but ending on a wavering note. Her eyes started to glisten as she brought her hands up to her chest and knotted her fingers. "I'm so grateful that you'll have that criminal locked up, so I don't have to worry about him taking another shot at me or hurting someone I love in the process."

Levi slowly took a couple of steps closer to

her and then waited. What he wanted to do was wrap his arms around her, hold her close, wait while she fell apart if that's what she needed to do and then reassure her while she pulled herself back together.

But he held himself back. This was something she needed to work through. And he knew how important it was to let her do that. Sometimes the most powerful thing you could do for someone was to just listen.

She sighed deeply. "I'm grateful that having this lunatic locked up means Grandpa and Rosa and Pablo can get back to readying the ranch to open for guests. That the workers will come back. That hopefully people will book cabins there and the business will take off."

She looked at Levi and the tears started to roll down her cheeks. "It finally looks like things will be going the way I want them to. So how come I'm not happy? What's *wrong* with me?"

Levi's lips lifted in the barest of smiles.

Vanessa's eyes squinted with suspicion.

"I can't tell you how many times I've asked myself the exact same question," Levi said. "I've lived through experiences I wouldn't wish on anybody. Just like you have. You want to believe one answer or one good break where things finally go your way will make all of the bad things feel resolved in an instant. Sometimes that's not the case. It takes time to work through it all. You have to keep moving forward. And don't be so hard on yourself."

All of those words were things other people, particularly counselors, had told Levi repeatedly after he'd returned home from combat. He'd thought coming home would be the best feeling in the world, and he'd been shocked to find himself feeling miserable shortly after he'd gotten back.

Looking at Vanessa, he realized how much going through these experiences with her the last few weeks had helped those words to sink in and take hold in his own heart. He couldn't pay back all of those people who had helped him. But as a cop, he could continue to help others and pay it forward.

He ached to wipe away the tears on her cheeks, but he commanded himself not to do it. That would not be professional. And the last thing he needed to do right now was confuse either one of them about the nature of their relationship. He was a cop helping a citizen who'd needed his assistance.

But she kept her gaze locked on his. She took one step toward him, and then another.

Until finally she stood with her cheek pressed against his chest.

Of course, then he wrapped his arms around her. What else could he do? And for the moment, he cleared his mind of everything except for the warm feeling of holding her close and the realization that there was at least one person who knew the real, unheroic, imperfect Levi Hawk and seemed to like him anyway.

He stood there determined to hold her for as long as she wanted. Because he knew full well she was returning to her life in Las Vegas and he wouldn't get the opportunity to hold her again.

Vanessa sat on the top rail of the corral fence, watching her grandpa as he brushed Maybelle. The old horse snorted and happily tossed her head back a couple of times as though trying to let him know that the brush was hitting the right spot.

"It's just not enough," Vanessa said, picking up the thread of the conversation they'd been having all morning. "Didn't you think that knowing who killed Dad and seeing him finally locked up would feel a lot more, I don't know, satisfying? Like something to celebrate?"

Grandpa stopped brushing and turned around

to look at her. "I am celebrating. I'm thanking the good Lord that the criminal who's been targeting my favorite granddaughter is locked up."

"Are you saying I'll get that feeling of celebration or peace or whatever it is I'm looking for after Goren is charged with Dad's murder? Or maybe after he's convicted?"

She thought about what Levi had said. That she needed to give herself time to adjust to it all.

Yesterday morning, at just about sunrise, Levi had driven her home from the police station. Grandpa, Rosa and Pablo had all been in the front room waiting for them. Pablo had made a big breakfast. Tornado had grabbed a piece of cheddar cheese from the cutting board on the kitchen counter and darted away as fast as his little kitty paws could take him. Other than that, the meal had been peaceful and it had given them all a chance to talk about the night's events and unwind.

Vanessa had found herself wondering if there was still a second shooter at large, but she hadn't mentioned it. She'd been terrified at the time the bullets were flying and she couldn't trust herself to accurately remember every detail of all that had happened. And she didn't want her family spending the rest of their lives worrying about a phantom shooter that might not have ever existed.

Grandpa had insisted Levi catch a few hours of sleep at the ranch house rather than drive all the way back to his own home after having been up all night. With Goren arrested, there really wasn't any reason for Levi to stay at the ranch anymore.

Vanessa had slept until early afternoon. When she got up, Levi had already gone back to the police station. She was both disappointed and relieved. She'd thought about him as soon as she'd woken up and wanted to see him. But if he'd been around, who knew what kind of foolish thing she might have said to him. Her emotional reaction to the man was getting a little out of hand.

Levi had returned with her to the ranch late last night and stayed in his room there when he could have gone home now that her attacker had been locked up and she was safe. An action she found kind of interesting. And he'd gone back to work again very early this morning.

Was there really any point in her continuing to deny the connection she felt with Levi? It was unlike any other relationship she'd ever had with a man. Sure, she'd been attracted to other guys, only to have things fizzle out.

And she had male friends. Good, solid, reliable friends. But they would never be anything more than friends.

With Levi, it felt like their relationship could go in a different direction. Exactly which direction and how far, she wasn't sure. That was uncharted territory. For her, anyway. Was she willing to take a risk and let herself see where a relationship between the two of them might lead? Was *he*?

"Maybe we'll feel happy, or relieved, or something like a combination of the two once Goren is convicted of Josh's murder," Sam said after thinking over Vanessa's last question for a few minutes. "Then again, maybe we won't ever feel that way. Maybe what we need to do is keep our focus on gratitude for what we have in the here and now. And keep hope alive for what might lie ahead."

"Really?" Vanessa pushed off the fence and stood inside the corral with him. Disappointment made her mood murky despite the beautiful day. After all she'd been through, she deserved an emotional payoff. Grandpa did, too. "I am grateful. But I want something more."

Sam stood with his hand on his beloved old horse, patting and scratching her while she chuffed happily a couple of times. Vanessa walked up closer to them and she couldn't help noticing how much her grandpa had aged in a short amount of time. He looked like he was ten years older in only the last ten months.

He certainly had the right to emotionally deal with Goren's arrest however he needed to.

Vanessa felt a stab of guilt and regret. She shouldn't have snapped at him. But before she could apologize, he spoke up.

"You might get that feeling you want eventually," Sam said simply, showing no signs of being irritated with her grumpy attitude. "But don't let your craving for it go too far. Don't let yourself decide that what you need is to see Goren absolutely destroyed. Don't get me wrong. It was my son who was murdered. I want to see justice served. But there's a reason why vengeance doesn't belong to us. For one thing, if we chase after it, it will eat us up alive." He brushed his hands together to knock off some of the horsehair. "It would never be enough, and it would turn us into something awful in the process."

"But, Grandpa..." And she stopped there because she didn't know what more to say.

"I want to see this guy locked up for the rest of his life if he killed your dad *and* for what he did to you," Sam said. "And when it happens, I'm sure I'll take some grim sense of satisfaction away from that. I imagine you'll feel the same way then, too. But I also want us to have other things to live for. I want *you* to have other things to live for. Other things that give you joy."

They left Maybelle in the corral and headed back to the house. As they walked, Vanessa found herself wondering how Levi would weigh in on the conversation she and Grandpa had just had. Maybe this was something he'd had to deal with, as a combat veteran or a cop. This weird feeling that real life lacked a moment when she could let go of all the old sad feelings and experience joy that everything was resolved. The sadness seemed determined to linger. Perhaps he'd found a way to come to terms with it.

She smiled at the thought that she actually knew somebody she could talk to about something like this. Somebody who wouldn't get panicky about such an intense topic and try to change the subject. Somebody who didn't see her as freaky, because oftentimes the serious topics of life interested her more than the lighter, mindlessly entertaining ones did.

Up on the front porch near the entrance to

the house, Sofia was stretched out in a patch of sunlight between two flowerpots. When Vanessa reached down to scratch her head, the tortoiseshell responded with an old kitty meow that sounded a lot like a gate hinge creaking.

Inside, the mouthwatering smell of enchiladas wafting from the kitchen made Vanessa realize how hungry she was. Her mind stayed on food until she walked past the small downstairs room where Levi had been staying. She glanced over and saw how neat and tidy everything looked. His bed was made. His duffel bag sat on the floor, looking like it was stuffed full of clothes. No toiletries on the dresser top. Everything packed up and ready to go.

Well, of course it was. Why wouldn't he be leaving? His mission here at the ranch was over.

As was Vanessa's, at least for the time being.

Her heart rose up in her throat at the thought of leaving everyone here and going back to Las Vegas. But that was ridiculous. She had to go home. That had been the plan all along.

She was fortunate her employer had been so accommodating. But working from the ranch was only a temporary arrangement. She'd been hired to do battle in courtrooms in Las Vegas. And she needed that paycheck if she was going to send money back here to keep the guest ranch from going under. Especially for the stretch of time it would take for guests to get past their fear of potentially getting shot at.

Once she caught up on her workload, she'd be back for visits. And of course, she'd return for Kenny Goren's trial. Unless he accepted a plea deal and there was no trial. Which would be disappointing.

Either way, her grandpa was right. She needed to get her thoughts focused on doing things that were constructive and building a future for herself. While her heart might be here in Torchlight, her life was going to be in Las Vegas.

"I could have been wrong." Vanessa turned to Levi while she dried the dinner dishes. "There probably wasn't a second shooter. Goren probably fired a few rounds, got frustrated because he missed me and moved his position a little thinking that would help him hit his target. And he'd brought a second weapon with him so he fired that one, too."

"What if you were right?" Fear pulsed in the pit of Levi's stomach. It had first shown up shortly after Goren had refused to be cooperative in the interrogation room and laughed at the idea that he'd had an accomplice. Since then Levi had been afraid that Vanessa would return to her normal life in Vegas and the second shooter, still at large, would follow her there.

He'd spent every waking moment in the nearly forty-eight hours since then trying to figure out the identity of the potential second shooter and he hadn't been able to do it. Now he was trying to convince Vanessa to hide out at the ranch for a while longer until he was absolutely certain there wasn't another shooter, and she wouldn't listen to him.

She was heading back to Vegas tomorrow. He was moving back to his own home tonight. There wasn't much time to change her mind.

Rosa and Pablo had cooked a farewell dinner and it had probably been delicious. He couldn't say for certain. He'd barely tasted it. The surprising announcement that Vanessa was leaving so soon had killed his appetite.

With the news of Goren's arrest now public, Rosa had called the construction manager for the new guest ranch buildings who had in turn called his workers. Everybody was willing to be back on-site early next week. She'd also put the website back online and reconnected the links that would allow people to make reservations.

By outward appearances, the dust had settled and everything here at the Silver Horse Guest Ranch was back on track.

But Levi wasn't ready to let Vanessa go. He wasn't certain she would be safe. And, selfishly, he would miss his evenings spent here at the ranch. With her.

Okay, he could admit that his reasons for not wanting her to leave were personal as well as professional concerns. But trying to approach that subject with her now, after the assaults she'd endured and the heartbreak that had been renewed when she'd had to talk about her father's murder over and over again, just seemed *wrong*.

Vanessa finished drying the roasting pan, opened up a lower cabinet door and put the pan away. "Say for argument's sake there was a second shooter. I really doubt he'd track me to Las Vegas. What would be the point? I didn't see him so I can't identify him."

Levi was a little unnerved that she was talking about it in such a detached manner. Like she was arguing the point in front of a jury rather than talking about her own life.

She shook her head. "I know you said Goren

still isn't talking, but I think he murdered my dad and he tried to scare me away and then tried to kill me because he didn't want my dad's case reopened. Well it's too late now. It's a very active case. Again, I see no point in someone shooting me.

"Finally, as soon as the police department and the county prosecutor put the real pressure on Goren and he realizes he's up against murder charges and not just the assaults on me, I'm sure he'll take a plea bargain as fast as he can and rat out everybody he can think of."

"So just wait until then," Levi said hopefully.

"I can't." She glanced in the direction of the den where the others had gone to watch TV and lowered her voice. "I need to get back to work, so Grandpa and Rosa and Pablo don't lose all of this. They don't own it all outright. The mortgage payments need to be made."

The landline phone rang. Vanessa moved toward the phone in the kitchen, but then they both heard Sam pick up the call in the den.

"A few days won't make that much difference," Levi said.

She shook her head. "We both know the legal system doesn't usually move that fast. And I need to get back to Vegas and lose myself in work for a while. I feel like I need to catch my breath. Do you know what I mean?"

He nodded. "I do." There wasn't anything else to say. There weren't any more dishes to dry. He'd drawn out the evening as long as he could.

Sam walked into the kitchen. "That was Robert O'Connell. Said he felt bad about the way your conversation with him and his son ended. Said it would be sad to let an old friendship fall apart because of some mistaken notions and wanted us to go up to his ranch for a barbecue. I told him next time you came up from Vegas we might be able to get together."

Vanessa nodded. "Sure."

That moment reminded Levi that his friendship with the family at this ranch was only recent. And that he didn't want to overstay his welcome.

He went to his room and grabbed his duffel bag, then took it outside and threw it into the back of his pickup truck. It would be a while before the repairs to his police SUV were complete. Then he went back into the house to say his goodbyes.

Everyone insisted on walking him out the door. Sam gave him a hearty handshake, clapped him on the shoulder and told him not to be a stranger. Pablo did pretty much the same thing. The two men then headed over to the stables to make sure the horses were all settled in for the night. The little gray cat trotted behind them.

Rosa gave him a hug and a kiss on the cheek. She smiled slightly at Vanessa before disappearing back into the house and closing the door behind her.

So then it was just Levi and Vanessa. His heart was heavy with the things he wanted to say. But his mother had been right when he was a young man and she'd first told him timing was everything. Now just wasn't the time. He could only hope that when Vanessa returned to Torchlight at some point in the future the time would be right to tell her how he felt. And that she would feel the same way about him. But right now she wanted to get back to Vegas and her normal routine. And he wanted her to have what she wanted.

As they walked to his truck, he scanned their surroundings. Her logical arguments for why she was safe didn't matter. He was still concerned for her safety and a little nervous about having her stand out here for very long.

"I'm not irresponsible or foolhardy," she said, seeming to read his thoughts, as so often happened now. “But I’m not cowering in fear, either.”

As they stood by his truck, he glanced over at her sedan to keep himself from staring at her and doing something foolish. Like kissing her. “What time are you leaving tomorrow?”

“In the morning. Probably around eight.”

“I’ll come back to see you off.”

“I’d like that.” She smiled and his heart did a slow, lazy flip in his chest.

Then he got into his truck and drove away. Because at the moment there wasn’t anything else he could do.

TWELVE

Vanessa swallowed the lump in her throat as she came down the stairs in the ranch house one last time.

She hit the last step smiling, determined that the ache in her heart wouldn't show on her face. Heading back to Las Vegas this morning was the best decision for everybody. And if she was beginning to feel like Torchlight was once again her home, well, that was something she could work toward in the future, when her salary wasn't needed anymore. If she could really adjust to living in a small town again after getting used to the bright lights and action of Las Vegas.

Although Torchlight had certainly had its share of action since she'd arrived just a few weeks ago.

On the wall beside her there was a mirror and she couldn't help catching a glimpse of herself. At least the bruises she'd had were gone. With the exception of a couple that were almost faded. And her poor injured shoulder was healing up all right. A small price to pay to find justice for her dad.

Kenny Goren. Having the murderer turn out to be the prime suspect from twenty years ago was still a kind of deflated accomplishment. Yes, the killer was locked up. But he could have been locked up twenty years ago.

She would have to trust that God had a plan with all of this. And she was ready to accept the peace that her faith offered her. She'd spent enough time trying to reason everything out. There were some things she'd never fully understand. And she could live with that.

She took a deep breath and blew it out. There was still one worrisome thought that disturbed her peace. Goren hadn't confessed. What if they had the wrong guy? And what if there really had been two shooters at the ranch and they were still at large?

A chill slid down her spine and she mentally shook it off. Fear of killers hiding in shadows could go on forever. It stopped now.

"Ready to go?"

Vanessa startled at the sudden sound of a voice.

"I know what you said about not wanting any snacks for the road," Rosa said, walking around the corner from the kitchen. "But I packed you some anyway."

She carried a paper grocery bag that looked nearly full. Vanessa had no doubt everything Rosa had packed in there was loaded with butter and sugar. She'd eaten whatever she'd wanted while she was at the ranch, but she'd have to be more careful once she was back to spending long hours sitting at her desk. Yet another reason she was going to miss being here at the Silver Horse.

They walked outside where Grandpa and Pablo were already waiting by her car. They'd insisted on kicking the tires, checking the oil and washing the windows. It seemed silly, but she knew it was their way of showing how much they loved her.

"Well, it looks like old Levi made it in time to say goodbye after all." Grandpa gestured toward the long drive, where a Torchlight Police Department pickup truck was moving at a good clip and kicking up some dust.

Levi had texted Vanessa earlier to tell her that he was caught up with work and wouldn't make it for Pablo's extraspecial goodbye breakfast with cinnamon rolls. She'd been disappointed but also relieved.

She'd figured not seeing him would make her departure a little easier. She'd grown too used to being around him nearly every day. And his acceptance of her just as she was made it too easy to drop her defenses. To just be herself. And that was something she could not do when she got back to her life in Vegas. It might be okay here, but it wasn't okay there. Not in the shark-infested waters of her law firm.

As Levi drew closer to the house, Grandpa decided the bright sunlight beating down was making the inside of Vanessa's car too hot. He got inside, turned on the engine and rolled down a window. Tornado, who'd been milling around on the stretch of lawn checking on what everyone was doing, jumped through the window and sat on Grandpa's lap.

Rosa gently bumped Vanessa's uninjured shoulder with her own shoulder. "See, nobody wants you to go," she teased. "Not even the cat."

Levi parked, got out of his truck and walked up to Vanessa. For a moment, her breath felt caught in her chest. Looking at him, she remembered the sense of strength and calm she'd felt when he'd wrapped his arms around her.

She could almost *feel* it. And if he took her in his arms right now, she was fairly certain she wouldn't be able to leave.

But then, he hadn't ever asked her to stay, had he?

Maybe she'd just gotten caught up in the high emotion of the investigation. Maybe this was the time for her to crash back to earth. Vanessa liked to think of herself as a logical person, but after spending so much time with Levi she'd become more emotional. It might be time to shake that off.

"I wasn't sure I'd get here before you left," he said.

Afraid the look in her eyes would betray her emotions—and at this point, she wasn't even sure what those emotions were—Vanessa quickly dug into her purse for her favorite sunglasses with the rhinestones on the corners and put them on. Maybe that would convey the message that she was going and it was time for both of them to move on to other things.

"I'm happy you made it," she said politely. She glanced around. Grandpa had gotten out of her car, taking the cat with him, but he wasn't going anywhere. Neither was Rosa or Pablo. If she thought anybody at this ranch was going to give the two of them a moment of privacy, she was kidding herself.

She walked over to toss her purse into the car through the open driver's-side window and Levi followed. Her move hadn't given them much distance from the three people desperately trying to overhear them, but it was something.

"Saying thank you doesn't seem like enough for all you've done for me," she said softly. "You've kept me alive. You helped me find the man who murdered my father. That's something I've wanted to do for most of my life. There were times when I'd lost hope that it was even possible."

"I'm happy to help," Levi said.

"I'll be back for a visit in a few weeks," she blurted out. So much for being cool about this.

A slow smile spread across his lips and the expression in his eyes made her stomach tumble. "Let me know the minute you hit town."

She giggled and it made her feel like an idiot. Tough defense attorney Vanessa Ford did not giggle.

Then again, now that she'd met Lieutenant Levi Hawk, maybe she did.

Not wanting to drag out the moment of departure any longer, she gave everyone a quick hug goodbye. Then she got in her car, steered it down the long drive and turned onto the highway.

Heading out of town, she thought of her dad and what little she remembered about him. And she hoped he'd be proud of her for not giving up on finding justice for him. She also thought about Levi. Now that everything was over and her life was settling down, she would have time to think. And who knew what that could lead to?

She thought of the handsome lawman and smiled.

For now, though, she needed to get her mind back on work. She connected the hands-free device for her phone and started making calls to coworkers so she could get caught up on everything back at the law firm.

Entering a stretch of highway that became a canyon-like passage between a series of hills twenty miles outside of town, she was talking on the phone when she heard a loud "popping" sound, like something had hit the side of her car, and it fishtailed a little.

Confused, she lifted her foot off the accelerator just before a second projectile hit a front tire. The tire blew apart and her car swerved to the left. She pulled hard on the steering wheel and slammed on the brakes, desperately trying to keep the vehicle on the road, but her efforts were useless. The car plowed through grass and dirt, past pine trees and down into a dry ravine where it hit one of the pines and finally came to a stop.

Heart pounding in her chest, Vanessa tried to catch her breath and said, "Don't worry, I'm okay," into her phone. There was no response. The call she was on had dropped. Possibly because of bad cell connection through this passage. She punched 9-1-1 into her phone but nothing happened. The call didn't go through. Stunned, trying to understand what had happened and trying to think of what to do next, she realized she smelled gasoline. And then she smelled something burning.

She looked around and saw wisps of smoke coming from the back of the car. The car had come to rest in a deep pile of pine straw. The dry pine needles were pressed against the undercarriage of the car. Particularly around the back end of the car, near the exhaust pipe, where the metal was hot enough to spark a fire. And that fire could quickly spread.

Her door was bent from everything that had hit it as the car slid down into the ravine, and she had to push hard and kick at it a few times to finally get it open. The car was tilted and she half fell and half climbed out. After stumbling a few steps, she turned and looked back. There was a bullet hole in the side of her car. And the smoke coming from the back of the car was getting thicker.

She had to get away from it.

But somebody out here in these woods had taken a shot at her.

Shaking from adrenaline and fear, she tried to think which was the smartest direction to go. But there was no reasonable way to make that decision. Meanwhile, the smoke was getting thicker and she was starting to see flames licking the bottom of the car. She needed to move, *now.* She started walking, stumbling along the ravine, uncertain of where she was going.

"I'm heading back into town right now," Levi said to Sergeant Ramirez, speaking on the hands-free device in his police pickup truck. "Goren is known to hang out at the bar at the Fargo Hotel. They've kept it open during the renovations so I'm going to stop by there now, talk to some of the employees and show them his picture. See if we can place him there the night of the attack on Vanessa. Maybe he'll show up on some of their security video footage for that night, too."

"Sounds like a plan. I'm stuck north of town for a while. This jackknifed truck spilled onions all over the road. As soon as I can clear the scene, I'll check in with you," Ramirez said. Then she disconnected.

With the help of other officers, Levi had scoured Goren's property and come up with quite a few stolen items. Whether Goren had stolen them himself, or bought them for resale, wasn't clear yet. But it had been enough to hold him in custody for the last three days and keep Vanessa safe. Now, to build a strong enough case to hold him longer, Levi was going to have to discover more evidence.

He hoped to use that evidence to pressure Goren into talking about his possible accomplice. Vanessa seemed to have convinced herself there wasn't a second shooter that day at the ranch, but Levi wasn't so sure. He kept thinking about the report of the two men fighting on the mesa near the spot where they'd found Josh's wallet. *Who was the second man?*

At the moment, they had nowhere near enough evidence for solid murder charges against Kenny Goren. It could turn out that Vanessa would know who killed her father but she wouldn't get to see him punished for it. The thought of that happening twisted Levi's stomach into a knot. Vanessa would be devastated.

He sighed. He missed her already. And his earlier doubts were gone. Now he *knew* his feelings for her weren't just the result of spending so much time together, or sharing an intense emotional experience, or something as witless and shallow as physical attraction. He loved her genuine concern for other people. He loved her determination to be her own quirky self. He loved her strength. He loved her sense of humor. *He loved her.*

That realization sent up an emotional flare that felt like panic. He took in a breath and laughed at himself. Something like an emotional rockslide was shaking up his heart and his brain. There was no telling how things would settle. Or if she felt the same way about him. A little flirtation like they'd just shared at the ranch was one thing. A genuine relationship was something else.

There was one thing he knew for sure, though. Spending time with her had brought about some kind of healing for him. Made him accept that there was truly very little he could control in the world. That sometimes he would fail at doing the right thing. And that was okay.

He got an incoming call from Chief Haskell.

"Got some bad news for you," the chief said as soon as Levi picked up the call. "Goren's been set free."

Stunned, Levi didn't immediately respond.

"His lawyer dug up proof that he was in town at the time of the attack on Vanessa up on the mesa. We can still charge him with dealing in stolen property. We've got a solid case on that. But we had to drop the assault and attempted murder charges."

Vanessa.

Levi's mind was already racing ahead with concerns for her. Goren had been furious at being arrested. What if he went looking for Vanessa to exact revenge? More terrifying than that, if Goren *hadn't* been behind all of the attacks, then whoever was behind them was still out there. Probably more determined than ever to silence Vanessa for good.

Right this minute, Vanessa was driving across a long stretch of highway through a vast, sparsely populated area, without much in the way of police presence. And she was completely unaware she was in danger.

"Levi!" the chief called out through the phone after Levi didn't respond.

His blood had turned to ice water, his focus

narrowing to only the mission at hand, which was to keep Vanessa safe. Levi had already slowed down and was pulling off to the side of the road so he could quickly whip his truck around.

"Vanessa just left for Las Vegas about twenty minutes ago," Levi said, his voice sounding calm and not revealing the fear that was gunning his heart like a race car engine. "I'll call her, but I want to catch up with her, too."

"Keep me informed," the chief said, and then disconnected.

Levi punched the gas and flipped on his emergency lights and siren. He called Vanessa. There was no answer and the call went to voice mail. "It's Levi. Call me. It's an emergency." He disconnected and then called her number again and again, disconnecting each time it went to voice mail, determined to get her attention the second she ended the call she was on. Or when she saw that she had a dozen missed calls from him.

A few miles down the road, he cleared the top of a hill and his heart sank. In the distance, he saw smoke. He hit the gas pedal even harder.

When he got closer, he could see that a vehicle had left the road. It had continued until it stopped in a ravine and was now engulfed in flames. He quickly called to have emergency services dispatched. And then swallowing back the sickening sense of dread rising up in his throat, he climbed down as close to the vehicle as he could get without getting burned. And confirmed it was Vanessa's car.

The worst of the fire had already roared through it and the flames were starting to die down thanks to the damp needles and green vegetation close to the ground. There was no way anyone could have survived it. Then he saw the bullet hole on the side near the back end of the car. Praying as he searched, Levi started looking around for any sign that Vanessa could have escaped the car before it had caught fire.

Vanessa hunkered down in a spot with a couple of trees behind her and some thick scrubby brush in front of her. She hoped and prayed the smoke from the fire would bring help in the form of firefighters. And that the fire wouldn't spread into a wildfire so big she couldn't escape from it.

Who had shot at her? She had no idea. Not a single one. But whoever it was, he was close by.

She patted the pockets of her jeans for the

reassuring feel of her phone and slid it out to look at it. Still no connection. She tried to place a call anyway, just in case. Nothing.

And then she heard a sound, kind of like the buzzing of a bee, but more metallic. It grew louder and she realized it was a dirt bike. Some extreme sports enthusiast was out here, riding the rough terrain where there were no trails. He or she must have seen the smoke and her car. They were here to help her.

Cautiously, she waited. The dirt bike got closer and finally she saw it. The rider was covered in protective gear, including a helmet. Though his voice was muffled, she could hear him calling out, "Hello!" as he looked around, identifying himself as a volunteer with the local search and rescue.

What a relief. Slowly she stood and the rider drew closer. He pulled off his helmet. It was Trent O'Connell.

Trent O'Connell? What was he doing here? They were at least forty miles from the O'Connell ranch. He spotted her and grinned as he killed the engine on his dirt bike. "Hello, Vanessa." Then he reached for a small walkie-talkie, drew it out of his pocket, and spoke into it. "Yeah, Dad, she's over here."

Robert O'Connell was here, too? None of this made any sense.

And then Robert rode up. He had a rifle slung across his back. Had Robert O'Connell shot out her tire?

The hope and relief she'd felt only seconds ago plummeted into dark disappointment and a deep fear that set the hairs on the back of her neck on end. "What are you doing here?" Vanessa asked, fear making her feel breathless.

Robert killed his engine and pulled off his helmet. "Oh, honey, I think you know why we're here. I tried to warn you up at the Heaton House, but you wouldn't listen."

Vanessa couldn't do anything but stare at them and blink. This didn't make any sense. Kenny Goren was the person who'd attacked her. He'd had that hammer from the Heaton House at his property. He'd flat out admitted he didn't care for her dad.

Robert glanced at Trent and then back at Vanessa. "It was an accident," Robert said to her. Then to Trent, he said, "Son, explain it."

Explain what? Vanessa took a small step to the side. Something was telling her to get ready to run.

"The gun went off by accident that night," Trent said. "I didn't mean to shoot your dad.

He was trying to get my gun away from me, but it went off and your dad died."

Trent O'Connell had killed her father?

"Trent hasn't had a drop of liquor since then," Robert added. "He'd had too much to drink the night it happened. He shouldn't have been driving. Your dad was trying to do the right thing. He got Trent to pull over and tried to take away his keys. Trent had a handgun. They struggled. The gun went off." Robert shook his head. "I was furious with him. Your dad was a good young man."

Now it was starting to come together. Trent had accidentally shot her father. They took her dad's wallet to make it look like a robbery. Robert and Trent were the two men Marv had seen fighting on the mesa that night. They had been at the spot to throw away her dad's wallet.

And Robert had shown such care and concern for Vanessa and her mom. Disgust was starting to make Vanessa feel sick.

"Trent is my only child," Robert said calmly. "The ranch has been in my family for four generations." He blew out a puff of air and shook his head. "It could have all been lost if my irresponsible son had gotten locked up for murder." He sighed and scratched his head. "Knowing who shot your dad can't bring him back. Why'd you have to start stirring things up? We couldn't let you keep going, get your dad's cold case opened back up again."

He was telling her everything. Cold dread had her heart pounding as she realized that meant he was going to kill her.

She took one more step to the side. Then she turned and ran, through thick underbrush, over rocks jutting from the dirt, aiming for whatever ground she could see where they wouldn't be able to chase her on their dirt bikes.

She heard both bikes start up behind her. She could hear them getting closer. She reached a thicker section of trees and veered off at an angle, desperate to get out of their sight and out of their reach.

In the distance, she heard sirens. She needed to get back to her car, to the highway, where she could get help. She turned in that direction, starting to run as fast as she could. She rounded a cluster of trees and then a hand clamped down hard over her mouth and somebody dragged her to the ground.

"Those two men chasing you are close by," Levi whispered in her ear. Then he removed his hand.

On the verge of collapsing in relief at the sight

of him, Vanessa whispered back, “It’s Robert and Trent O’Connell. Trent killed my dad.”

Levi’s dark eyebrows rose in surprise.

Vanessa reached for her phone. Still no sign of reception. She punched in 9-1-1 and waited. Nothing. She turned to Levi. With a doubtful expression, he looked at his phone. Then he shook his head and mouthed the word *no.*

He dropped his lips back close to her ear. “We can’t stay here. They’ll find us. There’s a creek close by. If we follow it, we’ll get back to the highway faster. And hopefully the noise from the running water will help cover up any sounds we make.” Levi drew his handgun. “Are you ready?”

Vanessa nodded. They got to their feet. Trying to move quickly and somewhat quietly, they reached the creek. Levi had to holster his gun so he’d have his hands free to climb down the side of the ravine.

Rocks and exposed tree roots slowed them down. Both of them stumbled as unstable stones threw off their balance or slick moss made them lose their footing, but they kept going. Finally, they moved out into the center of the creek, where the water was shockingly cold but they were able to move a little bit faster.

They pressed forward around a bend where they came face-to-face with Robert O'Connell standing in the middle of the creek, his rifle pointed at the center of Vanessa's chest.

They stopped in their tracks. Levi reached for his pistol.

"Don't do it!" Robert called out. "Or I'll shoot her right now."

"And then what?" Levi challenged.

Vanessa could see that Levi had actually obeyed and he was keeping his hands away from his gun.

"Are you going to shoot me, too?" Levi asked. "Are you going to add cop killer to the list of things you've done? Emergency responders have already arrived at the scene of the car fire. You must have heard the sirens. If you take a shot, they'll hear it. They'll find you."

"Get over here," Robert hollered, apparently for the benefit of his son. "I've got them." Then he spoke to Vanessa and Levi. "Nobody is going to catch us because I'm smart. I've kept my son safe for twenty years. As soon as Trent gets over here, we'll do what we have to do. And then we'll disappear. No one will even know we were here."

"They *will* know," Levi said. "They already do. Vanessa told me you two were behind everything as soon as I found her and I called that information in to dispatch."

For a second, Vanessa's gaze flickered away from Robert's rifle and over to Levi. He was bluffing.

She turned her gaze back to Robert and saw that his facial expression had changed from arrogant to worried.

Trent stepped out from the woods and appeared at the edge of the creek. He carried a handgun and pointed it at Levi. "There's a lot of people over by her car," Trent said to his dad. "If they get a K-9 out here, they'll have us in an instant. We need to shoot them and go."

Vanessa's heart rose up into her throat.

"When I draw my gun, you dive into the water," Levi said, his words barely louder than an exhaled breath.

Trent stepped down into the creek, moving toward them, and slipped on something. He threw out his hands to catch his balance.

The sudden movement spooked Robert, who turned toward his son to see what he was doing.

Levi drew his pistol and fired at Robert. At the same time, Robert took a step toward his stumbling son and Levi's shot missed him.

Vanessa was supposed to dive down into

the water. She knew that that was what Levi wanted her to do, so she'd be less likely to get hit by a flying bullet.

But there was no guarantee taking that action would keep her safe. Or that it would keep Levi safe. So she lunged toward Robert while he was distracted by Levi and shoved him hard in the chest, knocking him backward into the creek.

A shot whizzed by her head and pinged off a boulder on the side of the ravine. It was fired by Trent, who took a second shot at her just before Levi returned fire. Trent's knees buckled and he tumbled down into the creek, his handgun clattering on the rocks beside him.

Suddenly a hand shot out of the water, clutching Vanessa's ankle and pulling her down into the creek. Robert. She kicked at him with her free foot, trying to force him to let go, but he kept dodging out of the way. Then she realized he was using his other hand to hold his rifle up out of the water.

She lunged at the rifle and grabbed it. She got to her feet in the thigh-deep water and took a couple of stumbling steps backward.

Robert got up and started toward her.

She aimed the rifle and pulled the trigger. There was a blast and Robert froze in place.

The bullet hit a tree and a branch fell into the water behind him.

"That was on purpose," Vanessa said. "The next shot won't miss."

"Are you all right?" Levi asked, coming up behind her.

"Yes," she said. And all things considered, she meant it.

"Mind if I take this?" Levi said, easing the rifle out of her hand.

"Sure. You can have it."

When he stepped up to take it, she saw what must be Trent's handgun tucked into Levi's waistband. She glanced over at Trent. He was on the bank of the creek where he'd fallen. Shot in the leg by Levi. Not going anywhere.

"Thank You, Lord, for keeping us alive," Vanessa said.

"Amen," Levi agreed.

Robert just stared at them, looking pale and defeated. Levi gestured at him to start moving out of the creek toward the bank.

As they were stepping out of the water, they heard voices. And a dog barking. Sergeant Ramirez called out for Levi and Vanessa. Levi called back.

A couple of minutes later, a big-eared bloodhound on a long leash broke through the tree line at the edge of the creek and bayed in triumph.

Trent O'Connell's worry had been well-founded. In the end, they were tracked down by a police K-9.

THIRTEEN

Levi could hear birds singing and flittering between the tree branches despite all the noisy movements of the first responders crowded around the burned-out shell that used to be Vanessa's car.

It was only a little past noon. In an hour, everyone would be gone. In a few months, the area that had been burned in the fire would barely be noticeable. Eventually, there'd be no sign at all in this little patch of nature that Vanessa's life had nearly come to an end here. A cold ripple passed through Levi at the thought of that.

The reality, though, was that she was fine. Just up ahead, sitting on a big rock in a grassy patch of forest surrounded by some purple and gold wildflowers. He could see she'd tossed aside the blanket he'd draped around her shoulders after she'd declined his offer to have someone drive her back to the ranch. Followed by his suggestion that she wait for him in his truck. She hadn't been interested in that, either. The danger was over, and she was enjoying breathing free air.

She stood up when she saw him. Sunlight filtering through the tree branches glinted on her sparkly hair clip. He was amazed the thing had stayed on her head after all she'd been through. But then, he was amazed at her. And reminded by the situation they'd just survived that it was foolish to take anything for granted. Like the idea that sometime in the future he'd find the perfect moment to tell her how he felt about her.

The time to tell her was now. Even though it was awkward. He was officially working. And they both smelled like moss and mud from the bottom of the creek. Not exactly the romantic moonlit moment he'd imagined to tell her how he felt. But it was the moment they had together right now. Before she slipped away from him and resumed her life back in Las Vegas.

"What are Robert and Trent saying?" she asked in her lawyer voice. Apparently, she wasn't feeling the same romantic sensitivity as Levi. That was going to make the declaration of his feelings a little bit awkward.

But then, she'd made things awkward for him from just about the moment he'd first met her. Eventually, she'd had him thinking and talking about things he'd kept locked up for a while. More recently, she'd made him miss her when she wasn't around. Life didn't have quite the same shine without her.

"Robert and Trent are saying a lot," Levi answered her question, setting aside his own thoughts for the moment. "Both are confessing to your dad's murder and to the attacks on you after you arrived back here to help set up the guest ranch. Both are claiming they acted alone."

Vanessa lifted her chin. "But we know what really happened. Robert and Trent felt free to tell me the truth because they were planning to kill me anyway."

"That's right. And Trent's confession has details about the murder that his father's confession lacks. Details that match information in those cold case files we looked at. Things that were never made public."

"So Trent really did kill my dad when he was drunk and they were wrestling for the keys to his truck?"

Levi nodded. "Someone told Robert his son was driving drunk, again. Apparently, that was becoming a pretty common occurrence and a lot of people were worried about it. Trent's behavior had been reported to the police, but they hadn't actually caught him under the influence, yet. And his father wasn't taking his drinking issues seriously. Robert went to get him that terrible night but it was too late. He'd already shot your dad.

"They grabbed your dad's wallet to make it look like a robbery. Drove away from the scene and then got out to toss the wallet."

"And that was when the two of them got into a fight. Which Marv Burke saw."

"Yes. Robert shipped Trent out of town immediately."

Vanessa sighed. "So why attack me on the mesa? Why all the attacks afterward?"

"Apparently when you showed up asking questions, a lot of the locals started discussing the case on social media. People wanted to see your dad get justice. Robert saw that happening and was afraid people would come forward who might have witnessed something—enough to reopen the case. He didn't want Trent, his only child and heir to the family ranch, to get sent to prison. Not twenty years ago. Not now."

Vanessa shook her head. "But I don't understand why Trent is confessing now. To protect his dad?"

"He says he doesn't want the family's money to be wasted on an expensive legal defense. He wants the money and ranch to go to his kids. He hopes his estranged wife will move back to the mesa with them and they'll be able to keep their cattle business going."

"So all of the attacks were committed by the two of them?"

Levi nodded. "Robert came after you on the mesa with the hammer. Trent was actually back in town when you were attacked at the Fargo Hotel, but he stayed hidden. He's the one who knocked you unconscious there."

"And Kenny Goren?"

"The O'Connells had been out to his place. That's probably when they planted the hammer. To make him look guilty. He *is* guilty of fencing stolen goods. But not the assaults on you. And not the murder of your dad."

She took a deep breath and blew it out. And then a smile slowly spread across her lips. "Now I finally know what happened and why. And that the murderer will face justice. I can be at peace with that. It's what I wanted for so many years."

Levi felt himself smiling back at her. He couldn't help it.

Then he saw her gaze settle on his lips, triggering a fluttering feeling in his chest that really wasn't like him at all. He cleared his throat. "I've been thinking about applying for a position at the Las Vegas Police Department," he said.

Vanessa's smile broadened. She tilted her head slightly. A teasing glint appeared in her eyes as she stepped toward him. "And why might you do that?"

"Because I need to see you every day. Not just when you can come back to Torchlight for a visit."

She stepped even closer to him, close enough now that as he tilted his head down toward her, he could feel her breath against his lips. "And why do you need to see me every day?" she whispered.

He swallowed thickly. "Because you've stolen my heart."

"Oh, that's so corny." She let go a husky laugh and it made him nervous. "You are such a cop," she said, tugging gently at the badge on his uniform. "And if I have stolen your heart, *Lieutenant*, it's only fair," she whispered. "Because you've stolen mine, too."

Joy surged throughout his body as he pressed his lips to hers, felt her kiss him back and then wrapped his arms around her, holding her close. She fit perfectly in his embrace. And perfectly in his heart.

One year later

The scalloped hem of Vanessa's sparkly beaded wedding dress swirled around the tops of her peacock blue cowboy boots. She held her brand-new husband's hand and led him toward a group of friends seated at a picnic table not far from a row of parked motorcycles glinting in the vibrant spring sunlight.

The wedding ceremony had been held inside the big dining and socializing building at the Silver Horse Guest Ranch, but the reception was taking place all over the property. Vanessa had opted to skip the formal seating and speeches given from a head table. Instead, she wanted everyone to wander and relax, mingle and feel at home. She wanted her wedding day to be fun.

The year since Trent and Robert O'Connell were arrested had passed by in a blur. Chief Haskell had given Levi a leave of absence from the Torchlight Police Department, telling him he was welcome back anytime. Levi had then gone to work at the police department in Las Vegas so that he and Vanessa could spend some time together when they weren't surrounded by the drama of a police investigation. That had been important to him.

And yep, their love was real. She squeezed his hand.

"Hey, you two! Don't forget to eat," Pablo called out to them from the big chuck wagon grill where he was cooking burgers and steaks. Several feet away from him, atop an overturned box, Sofia and Tornado were eating something from a paper plate. Probably a little bit of steak, courtesy of Pablo.

Finally, they reached the group of friends Vanessa was aiming for and her friends got to their feet.

"Olivia!" Vanessa called out, hugging a woman with reddish-blond hair. "Lily!" She hugged a dark-haired woman with glasses. Then she grinned at the rest of the group. "I'm so glad you all came. I'd like you to meet my husband, Levi."

At the word *husband*, she and Levi shared a smile. And then he shook hands with her friends. "These are the people I told you about," she said to him. "They're part of a Christian motorcycle outreach in Painted Rock, Arizona."

"So those bikes are yours," Levi said, nodding toward the motorcycles.

"Yes," a tall blond man who'd been introduced as Nate said. "Do you ride?"

Levi nodded. "Yeah, but it's been a while."

"Well, you're certainly invited to come to Painted Rock and ride with us anytime you'd like. We're all looking forward to getting to know you. And I have to say, we were all surprised to hear Vanessa was marrying a cop."

Vanessa's cheeks heated with embarrassment. "Nate's a sheriff's deputy," she explained to Levi.

"Your new wife had it out for me for a while," Nate continued, grinning while he continued to needle her. "Really busted my chops."

Vanessa gave him a sassy wag of her head. "I was just doing my best to be a good friend to Olivia."

"You are a good friend," Olivia said with a broad smile. "I'm so happy for you. And this ranch is beautiful."

"Yes, it is," Vanessa agreed. "Business is so good I almost couldn't get a reservation here for my wedding." She glanced around, her heart swelling with happiness. Her grandpa was over by the corral, with Levi's three nephews. They were feeding apples to Maybelle, who'd had yellow ribbons woven into her mane for today's special occasion.

"Are you and Levi planning to leave Vegas and move back here?" Lily asked.

"One day," Vanessa said. "Right now, we're staying in Vegas. And we're waiting to see what the future brings."

Levi leaned over to give her a quick kiss. It made her toes curl.

Many of these friends had survived tough times, just like she had. Just like Levi had. Through it all they'd managed to keep hold of their faith. And to hope for better times in the future. By doing that, they'd all managed to learn an important truth. Even with tragedy behind you, there can still be good times up ahead.

This time she leaned over to give Levi a quick kiss. Her toes curled again.

Yep, good times. They were here right now.

* * * * *

If you enjoyed this story,
don't miss these other
heart-stopping romances
by Jenna Night:

Last Stand Ranch
High Desert Hideaway
Killer Country Reunion

Dear Reader,

Despite our apparent differences, most of us really do have a lot in common. One of those things might be a few lingering questions in the back of our mind that are not going to be answered in this lifetime. And that can be tough to deal with. In *Justice at Morgan Mesa*, Vanessa is searching for answers and justice for her murdered father. Faith sustains her during that long, difficult search. That same faith also gives her the strength to move beyond past tragedy and toward a bright future.

I hope you enjoyed spending time with Vanessa and Levi and visiting the Silver Horse Guest Ranch. I'd like to invite you to visit me on my Jenna Night Facebook page or on Twitter @Night_Jenna, where I mostly retweet pictures of cute animals.

Jenna Night